LOL LAND OF LEGENDS

LOL LAND OF LEGENDS

Second Edition

KATY ROSENSTEEL

Illustrated by Kaley Blackwell and Maria Gonzalez

Dedication and Acknowledgements

This book is dedicated to my father, Robert Joseph Rosensteel, Jr. MD, who made me believe I could do anything I set my mind to do. It is also dedicated to my husband and my children who were my first audience and believed in my book.

Thank you Michael Kelley for editing my first edition and helping me through the process. I'd also like to thank all of the people who have read the Land of Legends and asked me to finish the trilogy.

Map of the LOL

Lake District

New Camelot

Humans Hills

Mountain District

Town Square

Green Sea

In Betweenz

Isle of Elyr

London Bridge

Fairy Tale Land

Fairy Tale Lane

Yellow Brick Road

Fairy Tale Town

Great Meadow

Contents

I

THE CASE

Local lore said the cemetery was haunted so none of the neighborhood kids went in there. "Haunted" sounded more magical to Robbie than scary so he spent plenty of time in the small cemetery surrounded by the wrought iron fence. The gates were always open, the hinges too rusted to move. Near the back of the cemetery was a stone mausoleum with a large oak tree pressed up against the side of the ancient building. On most afternoons after school, Robbie could be found sitting under the old oak tree, drawing. The stone mausoleum was marked with the name Smythe. Robbie knew that Jeremy Smythe had been a wealthy landowner who owned all the land that was now Rosecrest City. He had lived from 1811 to 1861 and was buried in the mausoleum with his wife Jenny. There were 25 tombstones in the graveyard; some of the names so old and worn off, you couldn't read them. As a young child, Robbie's mother had shown him how to do crayon rubbings so he could read all of the old names. Even at that young age, Robbie loved being able to bring out something that otherwise couldn't be seen.

Robbie loved this old cemetery, maybe because it appealed to the artist in him, or maybe because he had born in it.

From his resting spot under this huge oak tree, Robbie could see the entire city. There were plenty of things for an artist to sketch. He could draw landscapes, buildings and even people. If he looked to the east, Robbie could see the tall buildings of Rosecrest City in the distance, the skyscrapers, the billion-dollar businesses and the expensive hotels with their views of Beflin Bay Harbor. He could see the huge museums downtown and the big theaters, including the one his mother was performing in this very evening. He could see Town Square—a large tree-lined park in the center of the city where the small old-fashioned stores were located—like Brown's Apothecary, which made the best root beer floats Robbie had ever tasted.

To the west of this park, he could see the one-bedroom rowhouse where he and his mom lived at the end of a row of similar looking houses. Beyond his rowhouse, he could see rows and rows of buildings that looked like they were all wired together with miles of clotheslines. Some of the windows were boarded up now that the huge old factory at the end of the block had closed. It sat vacant, except for the rats. The neighborhood had been both pretty and affordable eight years earlier when Robbie's mother, Gabrielle had purchased #418 Parkview with its view of the beautiful park across the street. It seemed the perfect quiet spot for a famous actress to hide from the public, after she had lost her fortune.

It was true Gabrielle Sartes was still a very beautiful actress, but few people knew how difficult it was for her to get a part anymore. Robbie knew that his mother remembered nothing of what happened to her during her accident on the night of his birth thirteen years ago. All anyone knew was that she woke up in a hospital on October 26th with a newborn baby, a missing husband, a huge lump on her head and a terrible headache. She had no memory of who she was or how she had gotten there. Even the paramedics who had found her in this cemetery one dark night with a crying newborn, said that she had been alone and was unconscious when they arrived. In fact, it was baby Robbie's screams which likely saved his mother's life. At the hospital, the night nurse recognized Gabrielle from "Phantom of the Opera" and called the theater. Her agent, Rosalie came and took her home a few days later, helping her with the newborn while Gabrielle healed her body and her heart, but not her mind. After several long months, Gabrielle hadn't regained her memory, and it became clear that she could no longer star as the leading actress in wonderful new plays. Thankfully, she and her agent realized she could still get roles in plays she had memorized as a child, or ones she had performed before. On stage, Gabrielle was still glamorous. Off stage, Gabrielle hid herself away in her small home with her son and the lovely park across the street.

There were so many interesting things in the park to keep an artist like Robbie busy. He would sit under his tree and draw the teenage boys playing in the basketball courts with no nets on the baskets. He drew the smaller boys and girls throwing around a baseball. Robbie drew the little girls who were playing hopscotch, or jumping rope on the pavement. Robbie tried playing basketball with the other boys when he was younger, but the older and taller boys would keep the balls away from the shorter ones until Robbie gave up and walked away. He had joined in the game of catch occasionally, but not often enough to have to answer questions about why he didn't own a baseball glove.

Robbie didn't have much interest in basketball or baseball anymore. He preferred art. He was really good for a thirteen-year-old boy and had inherited his artistic ability from his father, or so he had been told. He had never met his father since the man had never returned to Robbie's mother after Robbie was born.

Robbie loved to sit under this big oak tree with his cherished art case, the one thing of his father's that he owned. The box was a wooden artist's box, ornately carved on every square inch of surface. It had a chiseled picture of a lion whose face and mane spread across the front side of the box. The rest of its body wound around to the back of the box and its tail wrapped around the remaining four sides. The handle was made of ivory. The carved grooves of the mane were so thick, Robbie could press his fingers down into the grooves. Inside the art case were oil paints, drawing pencils, an eraser, a small sharpening knife, pastels, a set of watercolors and even crayons. There was also a space to slide paper in behind the paints. Robbie spent a lot of time sketching with charcoal pencils. He preferred these for his portraits. However, Robbie had a particular fondness for color. Mostly, he carried the crayons for sentimental reasons, because they were his first medium since he started drawing about the same time he could walk. He was four years old when he had every color in the crayon box memorized. The big fat 64 crayon box that his Godmother Rosalie had bought him. He still loved the colors in the crayon box, but as he got older, he preferred to draw in pastels and sometimes watercolors. He liked being able to blend colors by applying one on top of another. He would mix the watercolors and come up with new shades that he would then get to name. He could mix colors for the most perfect representation of the sky, the bay, the side-walk, bricks, and even skin tones. Although he looked lovingly over the oil paints, these remained untouched in his box. Oils needed a canvas, and this was a luxury his mother said they couldn't afford. Someday, he would get one, but for now he was content with his treasured box. His mother had given Robbie this box on his tenth birthday when she declared that someone entering the double digits would be able to appreciate something so special. It was the only item he owned of his father's. In their cozy little house, he knew his mother had no room to store any of his father's former things. Besides she didn't like too many reminders of the man who had left them. Robbie, on the other hand, thought of his father all the time, wondering what the man was like. Those were the thoughts that kept him up at night.

"*Whack!*"

Robbie heard the crack of the baseball bat, followed by the shouts of the three boys playing baseball. Next, he heard the *thwack* of the ball as it landed on the ground next to him, right on top of his art case. He picked up the ball, and walked over to the fence to throw it out to the baseball players.

"Thanks Robbie" said the boy with freckles holding the bat.

Robbie waved at Fred and went back to his tree. Looking down at the ground, he dropped to his knees. Something was wrong! A piece of wood had broken off his fancy art case. In fact, one of the contours of the lion's mane had chipped off and landed on the ground next to the case. Robbie examined the box carefully and saw that this was no ordinary break! Yes, a piece had come off the box, but this "chip" appeared to be the lid to a narrow cavity! And the hole was not empty! As Robbie tilted the box back and forth, a fat crayon fell out of the hole. Robbie picked up the crayon and examined it, but found it highly unusual. It was not a color exactly, but looked more like glitter with a silver hue.

Hmmm. Robbie thought. *How unusual.* He held the crayon up and drew a vertical line in the air.

He liked the weight of the crayon and the way it sat in his fingers. Next, he examined the hole, which was now empty, but looked as if it could hold more than the one crayon. He picked up the chip and fitted it carefully back over the hole. He played with it until he saw how it would slide back and forth over the cavity. Then he tucked the glitter crayon away and stood up to go home.

"Ouch!" he said aloud when his shoulder bumped into something sharp. He could not figure out what he bumped into. *It appeared to be thin air!* He reached his hand out and waved it around.

"What in the world?" he exclaimed when his hand touched something in the air. Something that could be felt, but not seen! Robbie used his fingers to explore this thing in the air. This thing was linear. It extended about 12 inches from top to bottom, and if he wasn't mistaken, it felt an awfully lot like the fat line he had just drawn in the air.

To test his theory, Robbie pulled out that glitter crayon again and drew a small circle. He then reached out his hand to touch, and sure enough there it was—a small circle suspended in the air. He grabbed the circle in his hand and brought it closer to his face. He turned his hand every which way but could not see anything. But, he could feel it like a thin bracelet in his hand!

"This is weird!" Robbie said as he crawled right up to the line and bumped into it again. He stared right at where it should be, then crawled all the way around it studying where he thought it would be.

Then he stood up and looked again. The setting sun was peeking through the leaves of the oak tree and Robbie walked back and forth in front of the line. He thought he saw something! Fascinated, he moved his head this way and that until he could just make out shafts of light hitting glittering particles in the air in the shape of a line.

"Amazing!" Robbie reached out and grabbed the line. He turned it around in his hand like a baton. He knelt down and began to draw with this "stick" in the dirt. He wrote his name. Liking the feel of this new tool, he decided to draw a picture of his favorite oak tree in the dirt.

The sun was setting and he knew he had to get home before dark, so he placed the bracelet and the line in his art case and tucked the crayon into its secret cavity. He headed home confused but excited to tell his mother about the amazing new crayon he had found.

2

A NARROW ESCAPE

As soon as Robbie got home, he ran to his mother's room to tell her about his discovery. His mother wasn't in her room. In fact, she wasn't home at all. Then he remembered, it was opening night of *Peter Pan*. Gabrielle was playing Wendy's mother and didn't have a big part in this play, but it was tradition that he goes to all of her opening nights and watch the production from the wings.

He quickly changed into the clothes that his mother had brought home for him from the costume department. It amazed him how she was always able to sneak home a perfect fitting tuxedo for him before each play. He grabbed a sandwich as he headed out the door to the bus station that would take him across town to the theater.

For the next few weeks Robbie saw very little of his mother. She left for the theater before he got home from school, she came home very late each night when he was sleeping and was not awake in the morning when he left for school. Matinee performances were held on the weekends. Weekends were also the time when his "famous" mother arranged to be seen by the public. She explained to Robbie that keeping up this public image was very important to her career and their livelihood. Robbie spent much of this time alone entertaining himself while Gabrielle was seen at the best restaurants and elite boutiques with other actors and actresses. Hardly anyone noticed that she rarely bought anything while she shopped and none were surprised that the beautifully thin actress ordered only salad and water at the finest restaurants. Luckily, someone else picked up the bill most of the time.

Robbie was used to being alone, and he had his art. Now, he also had this new glitter crayon. Robbie tried to tell his mother about it a few times, but she was too busy to listen. When she wasn't absorbed in a play production, Robbie's mom was a lot of fun. Robbie loved spending time with her. She was creative and had a great imagination. They would act out plays from stories his mother knew by heart, like the Boy who Cried Wolf, Peter Pan and Little Red Riding Hood. Robbie's mom would create costumes out of pillowcases and scarves while Robbie drew scenes on the big pieces of white paper he got from the friendly butcher down the block.

After several failed attempts to get her attention, he finally just said, "Mom, I have this cool crayon in my art case that draws invisible pictures." She didn't even look up from manicuring her nails when she said, "That's nice dear. Why don't you make a nice picture with your crayons?" Robbie knew that she was likely to be in this fog for the first few weeks of this production so he decided he would keep his new treasure to himself for the time being. Once the "fog" lifted and his mother was free again, she was the absolutely coolest person to be around, turning everything into a game of imagination. He would show her how the crayon worked then.

Since the day of his discovery, Robbie had gone to the park every day and drawn something new with his glitter crayon. He drew a paper airplane, but spent an hour feeling around for it after he threw it. He drew a kite with a long string, but got frustrated when he couldn't see it flying. He then tried drawing more elaborate three-dimensional things like a chair, an easel and a toy car. He was pleased to discover the chair could hold his weight and not break when he sat in it. He became a little concerned about wearing down the crayon so he did not attempt to draw anything too big or too elaborate. He also discovered a problem in trying to store his new things. He slept in the living room of his house and had a small cupboard he kept his clothes and few possessions in. He decided he would tuck it behind the tree up next to the mausoleum in the park.

After all, it wasn't as if somebody would see it and take it, Robbie thought to himself.

"Hey Ed. How's it going?" Robbie greeted his CityBus driver for his long ride across the City of Rosecrest. While the bus driver usually looked in the mirror when he pulled the door open for Robbie, he rarely ever spoke and today was no exception. Ed was a good guy though, and a friend of Robbie's Godmother, Rosalie. This was not a school bus, but a public bus, and Robbie had been taking this route home from school for many years. Ed didn't report to anyone that Robbie was using his Godmother's address to go to the upscale Hudley School rather than the school in his own poor neighborhood.

A few stops later, after Robbie had taken his usual seat in the back of the bus, three young men got on the bus. They were wearing white t-shirts, black jeans, black high tops and black coats. Each had a white bandana tied around his right ankle. He didn't know much about the gang they belonged to, but his instincts told him to avoid being noticed. Robbie slouched way down in his seat and propped his knees on the back of the seat in front of him, secretly watching the men without drawing any attention to himself. Fortunately, they sat two rows in front of him and never looked Robbie's way.

As they sat down, the man with stubble on his chin said to the one with a shaved head, "Lemme see it man."

The bald man asked, "What, here?"

"Yeah, here. Not like anybody's gonna see it." Stubble said and glanced toward the front of the bus where there were only four other passengers sat, lost in their own thoughts.

The bald man satisfied himself with a quick glance around, then opened his jacket and pulled something out. Robbie had to stretch his neck to see what they had in their hands. What he saw was a gold knife with a fancy jewel encrusted handle. He was not sure what they were doing with it, but it seemed strange to see these thugs with something that looked like it belonged in a museum? Robbie couldn't help but wonder if it was stolen which might explain why the one guy was hiding it in his jacket?

Up to this point, the tallest man hadn't said a word. Now he turned to the bald man and slapped him on the back of the head and said, "Put it away, you idiot. What're you thinkin'?"

Robbie's bus stop was coming up soon. He tried to think of a way that he could get off the bus without drawing attention to himself, but he couldn't come up with anything. He made up his mind to ride the bus all over town waiting for these men to get off, only then would he make his presence known.

So why was Ed slowing the bus down...and stopping? Maybe somebody else requested a stop and Robbie didn't notice. He could hope. Now the bus had definitely stopped, and the doors were opening. Ed looked up in his big rearview mirror, right at Robbie. "You getting out today, boy?" he asked.

Thinking fast, Robbie blinked his eyes quickly, stretched his arms up and yawned, cracking his neck as if he had just woken up.

"Sorry Ed. Must've fallen asleep. Thanks," he said groggily as he got up from his seat. *Maybe my mother isn't the only good actor in the family,* he thought to himself.

The three men looked at Robbie as he passed their seats, then looked at each other.

Robbie breathed a sigh of relief as he heard the hiss of the bus doors close behind him. *That was a close one,* he said to himself and started walking. He expected to hear the sound of the bus releasing the brakes as it drove away, but heard a very frightening sound instead. The door was opening again.

Keep walking. Don't turn around. Keep walking. Robbie coached himself as he tried to remain calm. When he passed the first row of houses, he turned down the avenue and started sprinting as if his life depended on it. After a few more blocks and a couple of quick turns, he risked a quick glance behind him just to make sure he was not being followed.

But he was! The three boys from the bus were running after him! Robbie ran faster than he had ever run before, sprinting toward the park. The men were still following him, but Robbie had a slight lead and headed straight for the cemetery hoping the men would not follow him in there. Robbie ducked behind the mausoleum, and peeked over it. Just as he hoped, the bald boy who reached the cemetery first drew up to a quick halt and waited for the others. A few moments later, the other two caught up and asked why he stopped.

"I ain't goin' in there," he said. "I don't do cemeteries with all them spooks in there". 'Sides, this fence is pretty high so he has to come out the same way he got in. We can just wait for him."

Tall Guy slapped him on the back of the head and said, "You idiot. Go and get him. Ain't nobody in there but that kid and some dead people."

While Robbie watched them, he opened the cavity on his art case and reached for his glitter crayon. He knew he needed to draw something to help him hide, and drew the first thing that came to mind--a board, big and tall, right in between him and the three men. As quick as he could, he turned the crayon sideways and added shading so that he wouldn't be seen behind the board.

Good job Robbie, he thought to himself as he continued to watch the men who were staring in his direction at the back of the cemetery and arguing over a plan.

From behind the board, Robbie couldn't even see if the thugs had ventured into the cemetery, so he quickly drew a peephole. He looked out and saw that there was no escape route. With his board propped against the tree, the mausoleum on one side and the fence on the other, he was fenced in.

The boys were starting to circle behind the mausoleum and he worried they might knock over his board and find him. On impulse, he drew a knob to hold it in place, changing it into a door. He grabbed the knob, and held firmly. Robbie stared through the peephole and held his breath. The men were only a few feet away and Robbie's hand began to sweat on the door handle.

"Where'd he go?" asked Stubble who had arrived first. Tall Guy caught up and slapped him in the back of the head, and accused, "You lose him, idiot?"

"Naw, he's gotta be here somewhere."

"I'll guard the gate and you find him," Tall Guy said as he ran back to cover the cemetery entrance.

Stubble and Baldy started walking in Robbie's direction. Stubble was nearing the door, but Robbie couldn't see Baldy from his peephole. Stubble was standing right in front of him now, staring right into his eyes. Robbie started to panic thinking the man had seen him, but then he heard a scream. He knew he hadn't opened his mouth.

"Aaaaaaaaaaaaaaaaaa!" Stubble screamed and started running. This time, he ran straight through the gate and out of the cemetery.

"What are you screaming for, fool?" yelled Baldy who was still in the back of the cemetery.

"G-g-g-ghost" stuttered Stubble.

"I ain't seen no ghost," Baldy yelled back.

"Me neither," said Tall Guy as he slapped Stubble in the back of the head.

"Oww! I did see it. I seen a ghost. It was just eyes. Big silver eyes! No body, just eyes! I swear it!" insisted stubble, who was absolutely terrified.

"I don't see nothin'," Baldy said from somewhere near Robbie's hiding place. Then Robbie felt a tremor as Baldy walked headfirst into the invisible door.

"Ouch!" exclaimed Baldy.

"What?" shouted Tall Guy and Stubble in unison.

"I just ran into somethin', only I don't see nothin' there."

"Ghost!" yelled Stubble. "See? I told you it was there. Run."

Baldy did not need to be told twice, he was already sprinting out of that cemetery as fast as his legs could carry him. Baldy didn't stop when he reached the men at the gate; he just kept running. The other two men ran after him and didn't stop running until they were out of sight. The three thugs never turned back to look at the haunted cemetery.

Hearing their scrambling feet disappear into the distance, Robbie felt relieved and really glad that he hadn't wet his pants in fear. He slowly turned the knob to come out from behind the door. As he peeked through the crack in the door to see if the thugs were actually gone, he saw something completely unexpected. Instead of the roof of the mausoleum and the brown dirt at its base, Robbie saw a bright green grassy field. He opened the door all the way and saw a wide meadow with the greenest grass and bluest sky he had ever seen. It seemed to go on forever. He pulled his arm back into the hiding place and it was still intact. Confused, Robbie closed the door and crawled out around the board. Standing again in the familiar cemetery, he reached out and touched the invisible board. With his glitter crayon, he drew a knob on this side of the board and pulled the door open. What he saw was the big old tree and his recent hiding place. He closed the door and opened it again hoping to catch another glimpse of the green meadow, but saw only the tree. He tried again...tree. Again...tree. Robbie looked through the peephole...tree. Disappointed, he turned to go home. He thought to himself, *the grass is greener on the other side!*

3

THE OTHER SIDE

As soon as he got home, Robbie wanted to tell his mother all about his adventure, but Gabrielle was performing tonight, just like every night during play season. He really needed to tell her his story, so he decided to stay up really late and wait for her to get home. Lying on the couch, staring at the door, he waited for her, but by midnight his eyes were very heavy and fell shut anyway. When Gabrielle came home, she tiptoed quietly over to turn off the light next to the couch. She couldn't resist touching Robbie's cheek lovingly as she smiled down at her sleeping son.

"Mom?" Robbie struggled to rouse himself from his sleep.

"It's late, honey. Go back to sleep," Gabrielle said as she bent over to plant a soft kiss on his forehead.

"Three guys. Tall, Bald, Stubble. Stolen knife. Hid in Cemetery. Drew a door. Crawled inside. A ghost. Scared. Ran Away." Robbie tried desperately to tell his mom about his adventure, but his foggy brain was not helping.

"Sounds like you're having a bad dream. Go back to sleep, honey! You've got school in the morning." With that, Gabrielle tucked in the blankets and gave him another good night kiss.

"No, really mom..." Robbie struggled to get his brain working.

Gabrielle put her finger over his lips and said, "Shhh! No more talking."

Unable to fully wake himself up, Robbie gave in to sleep.

Robbie overslept the following morning and missed his early morning bus ride. When he blinked awake, it was 8:00, and he knew he should be at school already. He quickly yanked on his school clothes and left his house in a hurry. He walked to the bus stop thinking about how tired he was, which reminded him of his adventure from yesterday. He thought about the door and the mysterious green meadow and how crazy that sounded! Robbie started to think maybe his mother had been right and he had dreamt all of it. It didn't even make sense that he pulled open the door to see the meadow, but when he crawled out and pulled the door open from the other side, he saw nothing but the cemetery. *Wait, maybe that was it,* Robbie realized he needed to try opening the door again from the tree side. The next bus wouldn't arrive for half an hour so Robbie quickly decided to return to the cemetery.

The morning was gloomy and gray, with fingers of fog reaching over the tombstones, making the cemetery feel more scary than usual. Robbie headed straight for the mausoleum in the back and looked at the spot he thought the door would be, but he saw nothing. He stuck out his arm and felt nothing. He waved it back and forth and still felt nothing. Just then the clouds shifted and a shaft of sunlight shot out. The bright rays of the sun struck something in front of Robbie, but down by his legs. He saw the glittery outline of a door, his door. It was still there but had tilted onto its side. He reached out and set it up, nestling it into the corner between the tree and the mausoleum. On second thought, he turned the door over so the inside was facing out.

When he opened the door, he gasped. There it was! That beautiful green grass! It was like a sea of emeralds tumbling over a large meadow with rolling hills. Satisfied that he had not dreamt all of yesterday's adventures, and knowing that he would have to rush to catch the bus, Robbie started to close the door. He took one last look and saw a white horse gallop across that beautiful field.

What a beautiful white horse, he thought to himself. *I wish I had time to draw it, with its lovely silver mane and tail, its blue eyes and its single horn right in the middle of its beautifully shaped head.* Then he caught himself and held the door a moment longer. *Single horn...it's a unicorn?* Robbie forgot everything else as he tried to get a better look at that horse. *If only it would slow down a little.* As if he heard, the horse slowed as it neared a small copse of trees off to the left.

Mesmerized, Robbie stepped through the doorway with his ever-present art case in hand and calmly walked toward the unicorn—if, in fact, it was a unicorn. With each step across the bright green grass, his bravery grew. He started to jog toward the horse, wanting to see it up close. Nearing the copse of trees, the horse only a few yards in front of him, facing away as it munched on the luscious green grass, Robbie approached the beast slowly.

From this angle, he couldn't see its head (and the horn he thought he'd seen), so he slowly circled the horse, trying not to scare it off. SNAP! He stepped on a twig and spooked the horse. It threw its beautiful head into the air and galloped off again. Robbie ran after it. He just *had* to see.

The emerald field felt endless. With the art case tucked under his arm, Robbie ran and ran until he felt his lungs would burst. Eventually, he had to slow down to catch his breath. His heart pounding in his chest, Robbie looked back. The little group of trees where he'd startled the horse looked so far away—it was barely visible at this distance. He couldn't see the horse either. It had gotten away. Robbie leaned against a tree to think.

This is unreal! he said to himself. *First the glitter crayon, then the door, then the unicorn.... What next?*

Robbie stood thinking about his options. He could continue to seek out that strange horse. It had to stop running eventually. He felt silly now, *It had to be a horse. Of course, it can't be a unicorn. There are no such things as unicorns.*

There are *no such things as unicorns,* he insisted to himself. *But then again, there are no such things as glitter crayons that draw prismatic objects in three dimensions or imaginary doors that open into...what...an alternate reality? A fifth dimension?* Robbie had no answers.

He decided to return back to the door, but he realized that he had raced after the "unicorn" without marking the door's location. He remembered the door was a hundred yards or so from the copse of trees. Looking around to get his bearings, he used the moss at the base of the tree to decide the door was to the north of the trees.

Returning from the direction he had come, Robbie searched the area for over an hour but had no luck locating the door. His search started randomly, then he systematically searched in rows, like his mother vacuumed the carpet, but he had no luck. He didn't leave lines in the meadow like the vacuum left in the carpet so he couldn't tell how straight he was walking. Besides, he was looking for an *invisible* door. Tired, frustrated and beginning to get homesick, Robbie sat down in the grass.

To the south were the trees, and the emerald green meadow stretched west ending in a huge forest. A bubbling brook was to his east, and to the north he saw some haystacks and sheep grazing.

Thinking the sheep might lead him to a farm, Robbie headed for the haystacks. Nearing the quietly grazing sheep, he noticed a spot of blue--cornflower blue, just like the crayon in his art case, leaning up against the haystacks. Even nearer now, he saw that the blue patch was part of a sleeve—the sleeve of a shirt tucked into denim blue pants. Carolina blue socks and navy-blue sneakers completed the outfit. Sticking out of the top of the shirt was the head of a boy...a teenage boy with a navy-blue hat and a horn around his neck. The boy was asleep.

"Hey," Robbie said, trying to wake the boy. The boy didn't budge. He appeared to be fast asleep.

"Hey!" Robbie said louder this time as he nudged the boy's shoe, not too gently either.

"Hey yourself!" the boy said as his blue topaz eyes popped open. "I don't know you," he said as he studied Robbie. "You must not be from around here, because I know everyone around here and I don't know you. So, who are you?"

"Robbie. I'm from Rosecrest City," Robbie replied.

"Rosecrest City? Never heard of that," the boy said, "Where is it?'

Robbie paused, *What should he say? He hadn't figured out where he was? Or how he had gotten to this...this what? Fifth dimension?* "What's your name?" Robbie said instead.

"LBB, or Blue, if you like," Blue said as he stood up. His hat slid off his head as he stood up from the haystack. Blue reached down to pick up his forest green hat.

"Wait!" Robbie yelled.

"What?" Blue said, pausing with his hand hovering over his hat.

"Your hat was blue, navy blue just like your shoes. Now, it's forest green. What's up with that?"

Blue grabbed the hat back and shoved it on his head. It promptly returned to the previous navy blue color. "As I was saying, my name is LBB, Little Boy Blue. I watch the sheep and the cows for the farmer, the farmer in the dell."

Robbie's eyes got big. This was bringing back childhood memories of nursery rhymes his mother used to read to him. "Come again?" Robbie questioned.

"Never mind. What did you say you were doing here?" Blue asked.

Seeing no other option if he wanted help getting home, Robbie decided to risk telling the truth, even if it sounded crazy. He told him all about the invisible door and running after the horse, or unicorn.

"You mean Eunice," Blue said.

"What?" Robbie asked confused.

"Eunice. The unicorn's name is Eunice."

"I knew it was a unicorn! So, what about the rest of it? The glitter crayon? The invisible door? How did I get here? And where, exactly, is 'here'?"

"I can't answer most of those questions, but I can tell you that you are in the Ello El. Now tell me more about this glitter crayon."

Robbie laid his art case on the haystack to take out the glitter crayon, and Blue knelt down next to him, "Cool box!" Blue said as he gently traced the woodcarvings with his finger.

"Thanks. It used to be my father's. He was an artist, like me, only he left my mom when I was born and so I've never met him. I guess I should hate him for deserting us, but a guy with an amazing box like this couldn't be all bad. I just don't know why he left it behind when he took off."

Robbie didn't have a friend his own age and had never told anyone else so much about himself. He was too busy keeping the family secrets like his mother had taught him, but for some reason he found himself telling Blue all about his treasured box and the glitter crayon, even showing him the secret compartment. "This is where I found the glitter crayon." Robbie said as he pulled out the crayon. As Blue watched, Robbie drew a line in the air.

Blue stood up and looked at the line from all angles until he could finally see the prismatic flecks of glitter caught by the sunlight. "Cool! What else can you make?" he asked.

Robbie thought about it for a minute. He looked at Blue with the big awkward horn around his neck. "What's that for?" he asked.

"I blow it when the cows get into the corn, to warn the farmer," Blue explained.

So, Robbie started drawing a small object with a string through it.

Blue looked at it, trying to catch the sunlight at the right angle, but even when the sunlight reflected off the glitter, he still had no idea what he was seeing. "What is it?" he asked.

"It's a whistle." Robbie held it to his mouth and gave a single sharp blow on the whistle.

"Stop!" Blue panicked and reached for the invisible whistle.

"What's the matter? It's just forced air coming out of a little hole after it passes around a little ball?"

"I know what a whistle is. You can't blow it three times in a row. That's my signal for the cows getting in the corn and the farmer will come running. If the cows aren't really in the corn, then the farmer will think it's a false alarm and he'll fire me, just like he fired the other boy."

"What other boy?" Robbie asked.

"The Boy Who Cried Wolf," Blue explained.

"You've got to be kidding me? The boy who cried wolf? That's a legend, a fable, a myth, whatever you want to call it," Robbie said exasperated.

"Well, sure. I told you that you were in the LOL, the Land of Legends."

Then it dawned on Robbie and he replied, "The LOL, not Ello El. Ohhhh! I get it now, but wait, you're telling me that this is the place where legends live, like they're actually real?"

"Well sure, legends, fairy tales, nursery rhymes. You have heard of me before, haven't you?

"*Little Boy Blue,*
Come blow your horn.
The sheep's in the meadow,
The cow's in the corn."

"Um, yeah, I guess," said Robbie, "but that's a nursery rhyme people read to their children, it's not based on a real person."

"Ah, here in the LOL, books are very powerful. The more a book is read, the more powerful it becomes and the more real the characters in the book become. If they're lucky, the characters can be 'inpilqued' like me."

"'Inpilqued?' I've never heard that word."

"Of course not," explained Blue. "Inpilqued is where a fictional character is so widely read, the character is created in the LOL as an immortal being."

"So, all the people here are from best sellers?"

"No," said Blue patiently. "The characters in the books must be timeless, not characters of the moment."

Robbie let that soak in as he looked at Little Boy Blue dressed in all the different shades of blue and he remembered something, "You didn't tell me why your hat turned green then blue again."

"That's just my gift, I guess, or maybe my curse. Since I'm Little Boy Blue, I must always wear blue. I've tried other colors, but as soon as I touch them, they turn blue. I have done lots of experiments and know that darker colors like red, green, and purple make dark blue colors like navy, while lighter colors like yellow and white make shades like cerulean and aquamarine."

Robbie was impressed that his new friend knew his colors, at least the cool shades of blue like cerulean and aquamarine. "Alright, now that I know where I am--sort of, how do I find my door? How do I get back home?" Robbie asked a little worriedly.

Blue thought for a moment and said, "A transparency detector."

"What's that?" Robbie asked.

"A transparency detector is kind of, well, kind of hard to describe. Think of it as a sort of metal detector that detects objects that are hard to see, like a pane of glass for a window or a lens from a pair of glasses--that sort of thing.

"Great! Where do I get one?" Robbie asked, finally starting to feel relieved.

"The Wizard. I'm sure he'll have one. He has everything."

"Okay then, let's go. The sooner I get home the better."

"Well, it may not be that easy," Blue said, taking a deep breath. "The Wizard isn't exactly known for being generous. People know that he is very wise, that he knows what is best for everybody, but he never just gives you what you ask for—something about 'spoiling the child.' Trust me, he won't just give you the transparency detector, he'll make you do something, something dangerous, scary, difficult, or maybe something that challenges your belief system. Maybe he'll make you pay some really high price for it."

Frustrated, Robbie abruptly started walking, knowing the sooner he started the sooner he could go home. He called over his shoulder, "There's only one way to find out. What are we waiting for?"

Blue smiled and leapt in the air, grabbing Robbie by the shoulders almost leapfrogging over him. He loved adventure, and sitting around watching cows and sheep all day was not the exciting way to spend a day. He often daydreamed about the adventures he would take if only watching cows were not his destiny. All too often those daydreams turned to real dreams when he fell asleep on the job.

4

FAIRY TALE TOWN

Just when he thought the emerald green meadow would go on endlessly, Robbie saw buildings in the distance. Could it be a town? As they neared the buildings, the meadow started to give way to small clusters of trees. Under one of the larger trees, Robbie spied a rabbit out of the corner of his eye. Robbie stared while he tried to figure out what was strange about that rabbit. "Why isn't that rabbit running away from us?" he asked.

"That hare is sleeping," Blue answered uninterestedly as he continued walking.

A little further down their path into town, Robbie spotted a turtle. Again, he thought it was acting strange. "If I ever saw a turtle that was moving with a purpose, it would be that one."

Blue said, "Of course. That tortoise is trying to win the race".

Robbie looked disbelievingly at Blue, then looked further up the path and saw a ribbon hanging between two large trees. This "finish line" was surrounded by animals of all types and sizes. This was the race from the "Tortoise and the Hare", another legend.

"What would happen if we woke the hare up and it won the race this time?" Robbie asked Blue.

"Let's find out!" Blue said mischievously. He picked up some pebbles from the ground, which turned blue, of course, and threw them at the tree shading the sleeping hare. Nothing happened. Blue threw a few more blue pebbles, even letting one bounce off the hare's backside. Still nothing.

Blue shrugged at Robbie, "Sometimes you can't change destiny. Come on, we're almost in town."

This town was not like anything Robbie could imagine. It truly was out of a book of fairy tales. In fact, it was called Fairy Tale Town. At one end of town sat a house shaped like a shoe packed with children hanging out of every window, waving at people passing. The main street was lined with quaint shops one after another. Robbie chuckled that the butcher's, the baker's, and the candlestick maker's shops were right next to each other. In the center of town was a beautiful fountain with a low stone bench circling it. Blue plopped down on the bench, giving Robbie a moment to take in everything. As he sat, he reached down to pick up a pebble to toss in the fountain.

Robbie watched as the blue pebble left his friend's hand and made a small splash in the water. He was starting to get used to his friend turning things blue. Joining him, Robbie reached down to grab a pebble of his own to toss in the fountain. Just to make sure, he looked at the pebble to see if it was blue. Of course, it wasn't. Robbie had to take a second look, because the pebble was pure gold!

"Gold!" Robbie shouted. The fountain was full of pebbles, shiny *gold* pebbles! Other glorious gold pebbles were on the ground surrounding the fountain. Robbie started filling his pockets, mumbling to himself, "Gold, lots, rich, poor me, rich, proud mom, nice house, more clothes, food, lots of food, so much food, steak, chicken, veal, cakes, pies."

When Robbie could stuff no more pebbles in his pocket and both of his hands were full, he pulled out his glitter crayon and started drawing a backpack shading it so the contents would be concealed. He stole a glance at Blue who was not helping at all. He realized all of the pebbles Blue picked up would turn blue, but they'd turn gold again once he put them down. So why wasn't Blue helping instead of rolling back and forth on the ground with his eyes closed, busting a gut laughing!

"Why are you laughing?" Robbie asked, annoyed.

"They're worthless." Blue managed to say in between peals of laughter. He stopped laughing when he saw Robbie pick up another handful of pebbles which disappeared into thin air when he dropped them.

"Worthless? What do you mean worthless? Is it pyrite—fool's gold?" Robbie asked in a panic.

Blue stood up, curious about the invisible object Robbie had made. "No. I mean they're worthless, worth nothing. There is so much gold around here, it has no value." Blue stuck out his hands to find the invisible pebbles and felt the exterior of the pack. He poked at the backpack that Robbie had quickly made while his eyes had been closed.

Robbie didn't believe what Blue had said. He thought, *how could gold be worthless in this strange land?* He put on the backpack and started walking down the main street, looking around again at Fairy Tale Town. Okay, so some of the lettering on the signs was painted in gold. Maybe the clock tower had a solid gold clock in it, and maybe the roofs were shiny with gold shingles. He just couldn't believe gold was that common in this town, but there was no mistaking it. Even the poor children living in the shoe were playing in a sand box full of gold sand! The more he looked around, the more gold he saw, including a huge gold castle on the far side of town with a gold watch tower on either side of the main building, where watchmen could be seen in their gold uniforms. The castle was surrounded by golden sidewalks, lined with golden columns, and enclosed by a golden fence with a golden gate.

Robbie looked at Blue and asked, "How can this be? How did gold become worthless?"

"Well, first there was Rumpelstiltskin."

"Rumpelstiltskin? You mean the dwarf who could spin straw into gold?"

"Yeah. Look around you," Blue said as he pointed to the fields outside of the town. "Lots of straw, and where there is straw and Rumpelstiltskin, there will be plenty of gold.

"But," said Blue, "That's only half of it." Now he pointed to the far side of town where Robbie had seen the enormous golden castle. "That is the castle of King Midas, ruler of Fairy Tale Town. Everything he touches turns to gold."

Robbie thought about this for a minute. "So, everybody can buy everything they need. There's no poverty, right?" asked Robbie

"Not exactly," said Blue. "There is so much gold, it is not used as currency. You need other types of currency—paper dollars, quarters, pennies..."

Robbie decided this was a curious town and he wanted to know more about it. As he came to the end of the row of shops, his eyes followed the road out of town.

He saw a row of castles, each as big as the next. Even from a distance, he could see the gigantic pillars, long flights of entrance stairs, creative shrubbery on the lawns, turrets and battlements on the roofline. The furthest castle had a moat around it. One of the closer castles had a horse drawn coach in front of it with beautiful white horses and a very spherical orange coach. Another house had seven sturdy ponies tied up in front of the house.

"Wow! Nice digs!" said Robbie. "Who lives in those?"

"Those are the castles of the Princesses who lived 'happily ever after.'" Blue said, "Name a story that ends in 'they lived happily ever after'".

Robbie said the first one to come to mind, "Cinderella."

Blue pointed to one of the castles. "See the pumpkin carriage parked in front? Cinderella lives there."

Fascinated, Robbie named another, "Snow White."

Blue pointed to the one with the seven ponies. "Right there, and it looks like the dwarfs are paying her a visit as we speak." You can't tell from here, but Sleeping Beauty lives in the next one. Beauty and her Beast and Rapunzel live further down Happily Ever After Lane."

Robbie chuckled at the name of the lane and could see that it continued on for a long while, with castles disappearing into the horizon.

"So how do we find the wizard?" Robbie asked, returning to the pressing subject.

Blue turned and pointed at the gold palace again. "See that gold path alongside the golden gates of the palace?"

Robbie nodded as he saw a path made of gold bricks leading out of town past the gold palace.

"We follow the yellow brick road," Blue said.

Robbie groaned but started walking again. "You've got to be kidding? You can't mean that 'Wizard?' Everybody knows he was a fake!"

"Not exactly," Blue explained. "He likes to put on a show with smoke and mirrors, but he is still very wise. He told his visitors how to find the thing they most treasured just by looking within themselves. We respect his wisdom, but sometimes get annoyed with his roundabout way of teaching us what we need to know."

Robbie knew that he would not be able to find the invisible door or even a transparency detector within himself, but he followed Blue down the golden path.

Robbie had lots of questions for LBB. "Are there other towns like Fairy Tale Town in the Land of Legends? Is King Midas the ruler of all?"

Blue explained that Fairy Tale Town was the only town on Fairy Tale Island. It connected to the Isle of Elyr to the west, which had Timber Town. To the north was the ungovernable land. King Arthur ruled the land on the other side of the ungovernable land.

"How does King Midas rule a land if he can't even touch anything without it turning to gold?" Robbie wanted to know.

"He's learned to live with his gift. He is highly respected in this land, affectionately referred to as *the Pilquer,* since he is responsible for the *inpilquing.*"

"So, how does someone get *inpilqued*?" Robbie was fascinated by the power of the written word.

Blue patiently explained, "He has a trusted guard whose responsibility it is to notice when a book is widely read by many people for over a decade. That is when the book reaches *pilquing* status. The guard then sends these books to the committee of princesses to decide whether the characters in the book are worthy of *inpilquing.* Then, the princesses recommend those characters to King Midas. If he agrees, King Midas writes the names down in the *Pilquing* Ledger and before the ink dries on the page, the person is *inpilqued* and standing before King Midas in the flesh."

Robbie was fascinated, but Blue was already thinking of something else as he asked, "Are you hungry?"

Since he had skipped breakfast, Robbie was definitely hungry. "Yeah. What time is it anyway?"

Blue shrugged his shoulders and turned off the yellow brick road onto a path that led into the woods. "Time doesn't mean much in LOL. There is no passage of time. We eat when we want, we sleep when it gets dark, and wake up when it's light. There is no need to keep track of days, weeks, years."

Robbie looked perplexed. "I don't get it."

"Alright," said Blue patiently. "How old do I look?"

Robbie looked at him, "I don't know, my age, maybe 13 or 14"

Blue smiled, "When did you first hear the story of Little Boy Blue?"

"My mom read it to me when I was little."

"And was that the first time she heard the story?" Blue asked.

"No, her mom read it to her when she was little." Robbie was starting to see where this was going.

Blue finished for him, "And she learned it from her parents, who learned it from their parents, etc., etc. So how could I possibly be 14?"

Robbie exclaimed, "Wow! Cool! So, you'll never get old and die?"

Blue sighed dramatically. "Nope, never get old. Never grow up. Never get my own house. Never have a job other than watching cows and sheep for the farmer."

When Blue put it *that* way, staying young forever sounded less exciting.

The boys grew quiet while they continued hiking through the woods. Finally, Robbie asked, "Where are we going, exactly?"

"Just wait. We're almost there," said Blue. A few minutes later, they entered a small clearing with a little house nestled in the center.

"Hey Goldie!" Blue called out to the blond girl in front of the house. "Ready?"

Goldie looked up and waved at Blue. "Hi Blue. I just saw them leave so things should be just right. Who is your friend?"

"This is Robbie," Blue introduced Robbie as they joined Goldie at the front door. They stepped inside and found a table set for three—three bowls of porridge with three spoons.

Blue told Robbie, "I like mine hot, so I hope you like yours cold, because that's what's left." With that he climbed into a great big hard chair and started eating porridge.

Robbie watched as Goldie climbed into the smallest chair and started eating from the smallest bowl. That left a very soft chair for him. He was hungry so he sunk into the chair and took a big bite of cold porridge.

"So, you're Goldilocks?" Robbie asked with his mouth full of porridge.

"Goldie for short," she said. "How did you meet Blue?"

Blue interrupted, "He popped into the Great Meadow through an invisible door. He's from the World Out There."

Robbie shot Blue a look of concern.

"It's okay. She's cool. We've been friends forever. You can trust her," said Blue.

"For real?" Goldie asked excitedly. She had always dreamed of the World Out There and what it might be like to live there. She, too, had longed to grow up, get married, have a house of her own, have children and spoil grandchildren." She had a million questions for Robbie and Blue.

They told her all about how Robbie stumbled into the LOL and was now unable to return to his world.

"If I know you, Blue, you already have a plan, right?" she asked, with a gleam in her eye and a smile on her face.

"Of course," Blue replied confidently.

As Blue laid out their plan to approach the Wizard, Robbie observed Goldilock's expression slowly change from carefree to concerned.

"Do you want to come with us?" Blue teased.

Goldie looked away.

"I'm just teasing. I know you won't step foot in the poppy fields." Blue reached out and squeezed her arm by way of apology, staring at her until she looked back at him with a half-smile.

Then he changed the subject, "So, how are the three bears?"

With that her whole face lit up. There was nothing Goldilocks liked to talk about more than the three bears, particularly Baby Bear. It seemed Goldilocks spent a lot of time at the bears' house, both while they were home and while they were out. As Robbie listened, he recalled the original story of the three bears. Funny, he had always imagined Goldilocks as very young since she fit in Baby Bear's things, but now he saw she was his age. Eyeing the chair she was sitting in, Robbie realized that a Baby Bear is nearly the size of a human teenager.

Goldie and Blue teased playfully back and forth and Robbie joined in as he got to know his newfound friends. All too soon, the meal came to an end and the mood got heavier as the boys said goodbye to Goldilocks.

The golden path did end in a poppy field, but Blue warned Robbie not to stop and sniff the poppies as they continued to the Wizard's mansion. Nevertheless, they still felt a little fuzzy headed when they finally arrived at the city limits and the gatekeeper peeked through a tiny window in the massive gate.

"Hello there, Beautiful. If I had known there was such beauty to behold in this place, I would have come by sooner. My friend and I have a most earnest need to see the almighty and powerful Wizard." Blue sweet-talked his way through the gate and the blushing gatekeeper led them to a very large room with a large screen. Robbie was glad that went a lot smoother than expected, and was grateful the young lady was sweet on Blue.

As Robbie watched the theatrics in awe, a huge wizard head with a booming voice began to speak to them. It was a complete smoke and laser show. Robbie looked at Blue confused and said, "I thought..."

Robbie didn't have to finish his thought as Blue pointed to the curtained off area to the side of the "stage." "We know," Blue said, "but the Wizard is truly brilliant with a wisdom esteemed in the Land of Legends. He also loves magic even though he is not truly magical which makes him cranky and resentful of intruders. If he wants to present his wisdom as magic, there is no harm done."

The Wizard boomed at the boys to "Be Gone!"

Robbie panicked, worried that this mission had failed, but Blue was not scared off easily, and he calmly went over and pulled the curtain aside. The Wizard was angry, but Blue smoothed his ruffled feathers with his trademark charm. Blue had an undeniable gift for smooth talking his way out of tense situations.

When Blue turned to introduce him, Robbie noticed Blue was very vague. There was no mention of glitter crayons, magic doors or the World Out There. He simply said, "This is my friend Robbie, and he would like to borrow a transparency detector."

The Wizard turned to judge Robbie, quickly realizing he was not one of the familiar residents of Fairy Tale Town. After looking him overhead to toe, the Wizard's gaze returned to Robbie's eyes. "Rather unusual, I'd say."

Robbie didn't know whether the Wizard was referring to his situation, his looks or more likely his eyes, which many people had told him were unusual, beautiful, mysterious, and rare. Robbie's eyes were lavender, which was rare enough, but there was a silver ring around the outer part of the lavender iris. When Robbie got really emotional, the silver ring became more prominent, overshadowing the lavender making his eyes look like pools of silver. His godmother had told him how unusual this was, but claimed she had met a few other people in the theater world who had "changing eyes". He had experienced quite a few emotions today and was even now worried, scared and anxious to get home, but without a mirror he didn't know what color his eyes were at the moment.

The Wizard ducked behind a curtain and his floating head appeared on stage. In a trance-like state, the head muttered these words that Robbie scribbled down in a sketchbook from his art case

Thine eyes have I seen once with mine.
A pair of two over this time.
Over the Hew Mondz Hills, below a peak,
There you will find what most you seek.

Robbie repeated the words loudly, but got no response from the Wizard. Blue could offer no response either. Robbie tried again. "Are you saying the transparency detector or the thing I am trying to find is below a peak, because I have not seen any peaks around here?"

The Wizard, still in his trance-like state said nothing and Robbie thought maybe he had spent too much time sniffing poppies. He asked again, "Do you have a transparency detector?" One finger appeared on the stage area in place of the head, and it was pointing in the direction of the entranceway.

"Come on," said Blue walking back toward the door. "Let's go."

"But..." Robbie broke his gaze from the screen and followed Blue to the entranceway to talk to the Wizard's assistant.

The assistant bent down and pulled off a piece of paper from a printing machine. Robbie looked at the paper that appeared to be a "bill."

One transparency detector $1,000

Robbie then looked fearfully at Blue and asked, "What is this?"

Blue shrugged and said, "It's his bill. I told you the Wizard doesn't believe in making anything easy."

Growing up poor as Robbie had, he couldn't imagine coming up with one thousand dollars!. He was beginning to fear that he would never be able to go home. He jammed his hand in his pocket, or tried to anyway, before he remembered they were stuffed with gold. Hope returned as he grabbed a handful of gold and held it out to the assistant. She shook her head as she opened the door for them to exit. Sadly, Robbie remembered what Blue had told him about gold being worthless.

"I guess this is your quest, to find the money", Blue said reaching into his pocket and pulling out a few bills. I have three dollars in my pocket, how much do you have?"

Robbie was surprised that Fairy Tale Town used the same currency as his own country, but said nothing about that as the hopelessness of the situation settled on him. Finally, he said, "I have no money. That's the story of my life. All I want is to go home, see my mother. She's my only family, and I'll never see her again." Robbie threw the useless gold pebbles on the ground and kicked at the poppies at his feet.

Both boys felt the fuzziness creep in at the edge of consciousness. "The poppies, come on!" Blue said urgently. "Let's get out of here while we still can."

They took off at a run.

5

MONEY DOESN'T GROW ON TREES

Robbie was discouraged by his useless trip to see the Wizard, the hopelessness of finding enough money to rent a transparency detector, and how upset his mother will be when he's not in bed when she comes home after tonight's performance.

Sensing his mood, Blue nudged Robbie and said, "Come on, I know what will cheer you up."

"Are we going back to the Three Bear's?" Robbie was a city boy who hadn't spent a lot of time in the woods so all the trees looked the same to him.

"Not this time." Blue said, not giving anything away.

"What's up with Goldilocks anyway? Why did she get so upset about going to the Wizard?" Robbie asked.

"It's the poppies. She got lost in the poppy field once and ended up missing for days before she was rescued. Now, she will not go anywhere near that field.

"So where are we going?"

Blue didn't need to answer as they had come upon a little cabin. It looked sort of like a log cabin except it was brightly trimmed in red and green and white. The whole thing sparkled like sugar crystals! *That couldn't be,* he thought. But there was no mistaking it, this house *was* made of candy! Huge peppermint sticks served as columns on the front porch. Red and green gumdrops trimmed the two front windows. The roof was made of candy bars with licorice outlining the roof. The sides of the house were plastered with rock candy in a variety of colors, caramel drops were shaped into shrubs, and a fence of lollipops outlined the front yard. There were a few chunks missing from various parts of the house and looked like they had recently been broken off. Robbie wondered what would happen if it rained. *Would the candy turn to mush? Wouldn't the sugar melt and the candy slide off the roof?*

"Good, I think they're home," Blue said, interrupting Robbie's thoughts. "Take what you want before we go inside. And don't worry, anything you take today will reappear tomorrow morning." Blue broke off a huge gumdrop that filled his arms and held a chunk of the licorice and chocolate roof under his chin, then banged on the door. As if he read Robbie's mind, he said, "Good thing it never rains in these woods."

Robbie hesitated and then pulled up a lollipop from the "fence". He started feeling like a kid in a candy store as he tried to decide what to take, then decided to taste a little bit of everything. With his arms full, he followed Blue into the house.

He recognized Goldilocks, who was so anxious to see them return from the poppy field, she gave them both a hug, which was awkward for Robbie, and not just because he was still holding all of the candy.

"She's like that. You get used to it," Blue winked at Robbie.

He did not know the other two people in the room, a boy and a girl. He looked expectantly over at Blue who had a piece of candy bar on his cheek, blue candy bar, of course.

Blue crossed his arms and issued a playful challenge, "Before you eat, you get one chance to guess who these people are."

Robbie felt the pressure. That candy was making his mouth water. *Think,* he commanded himself. *Okay, I can figure this out. It must be a fairy tale about a boy and a girl. Is the candy house part of it? There is one about two kids getting lost in the woods and finding a witches' candy house. What were their names?* Robbie thought hard but the names were not coming to him, he started worrying about the witch coming home. He looked around the room and his glance came back to that big pile of candy on the table. He wanted that candy, and he wanted to eat it and get out of there before the witch came back and locked Hansel in a cage.

"Hansel!" He exclaimed aloud. "Hansel and Gretel". He shook their hands as Blue introduced Robbie to them.

Robbie sat down to eat his candy and wondered aloud if the witch was dead.

"Not exactly," Blue said. "Remember how I told you we don't grow up, we don't leave the LOL? We don't die either. Dying in a fairy tale is just a convenient way to end the story. The bad guy dies and the good guys live "happily ever after". Our story is like a play. Here in the LOL, it is our destiny to re-enact the same play over and over again."

Robbie was horrified. "In the story I remember, the children...uh, I mean you two, are terrified and the witch is tossed in the fire. You have to live that horror for the rest of your life?"

Hansel shrugged, "It's just acting."

That was something Robbie understood. He said, "So, you do this every day? Will the witch be here soon?" Robbie looked out the window nervously.

"No, only for the *repilquing*," Blue answered for Hansel. "After a book has been *pilqued*, the King's guard tallies how often the book is read. When enough tallies are earned, the book is *repilqued* and we must re-enact it to keep the story alive."

"What happens if the book does not get *repilqued*?" Robbie asked.

Hansel's face reddened and he turned away. Gretel covered her ears as if Robbie had said a bad word. Goldie hung her head remembering something sad.

Blue explained somberly, "We don't like to talk about it, but if your book is not *repilqued* each quarter century, the *inpilqued* people cease to exist."

Confused, Robbie questioned, "I thought that *inpilqued* people were immortal and could not die?"

Hansel answered this time, "They don't die. They cease to exist. There is a difference."

Blue added, "More than a century ago, my friend *Ragadamon* disappeared before my eyes."

"*Ragada* who?" Robbie said, "I never heard of him".

Hansel answered, "That's the point. After his *inpilquing*, people forgot about him and he ceased to exist."

In an effort to move past all of the sad memories just stirred up, Goldie asked Robbie and Blue about their trip to the Wizard.

First, Robbie wanted to understand how Goldie knew to meet them at the candy house.

"It's not far from the poppy field and LBB comes here every chance he gets. He has a real sweet tooth for blue candy," she said as they all laughed knowing that any candy Blue ate would be blue.

"Tell us about the Wizard," Hansel and Gretel said together. "What did he want?"

Robbie gave Goldie a suspicious look. She shrugged guiltily. "Sorry I told them, but they are my best friends." She took Gretel's hand.

Everybody started talking at once. Goldie continued to apologize. Hansel and Gretel fired off questions about the Wizard. Blue started to relate what happened, but nobody could hear him over the sound of the other voices. Robbie stared at them in awe. He didn't have a group of friends like this. As he waited for them to stop talking, he took a big bite of caramel, and spent the next few minutes trying to get the caramel off of his teeth.

Finally noticing that Robbie was not saying anything, everybody else got quiet so Robbie could tell the tale. His fascination with the Wizard had disappeared as the burden of the thousand dollars hung foremost in his mind. He simply said, "He wants one thousand dollars for the transparency detector."

Gretel who looked to be about 8 years said, "I have $120 in my piggy bank, and you can have it all."

Hansel pat her on the head, "That's nice, but that's nowhere near enough money." The room was quiet as nobody else had any great ideas.

"Let's face it, it's hopeless," Robbie said. "As my mother always said, 'Money doesn't grow on trees!'".

Hansel darted a quick look to Blue, who broke into a wide smile that slowly spread to the girls' faces as well.

"Is somebody going to let me in on the joke? Why are you all smiling when you should be upset over my sorry state?" Robbie was annoyed at being left out.

Hansel spoke up, "Well Robbie, in the Land of Legends there is a certain forest, a forest where money *does* grow on trees!"

Robbie stared at Hansel to decide if he was joking, but Hansel nodded his head. Around the room, the others nodded as well.

"Well, alright!" Robbie felt like the weight of the world had been lifted from his shoulders. "So how do I get to this Forest of Money?"

Blue stood up, his thirst for adventure not yet quenched, "I'll show you".

"I'm coming too," Goldie chimed in.

"Me too," said Gretel bouncing up.

"Gretel, you're too little. Father would be angry with me for letting you go," said the more cautious Hansel.

"Just try and stop me, Hansel!" argued his stubborn sister.

Hansel knew arguing was no use. Once Gretel set her mind on

something, she refused to give up. “Then I guess I’ll be coming too, to keep an eye on you,” he said, giving in.

6

LONDON BRIDGE

It was late in the day when the group set off for the Forest of Money, but Robbie insisted there was no time to waste. He wanted to get home before his mother started to worry. With any luck, his mother would be so preoccupied with her performance in *Peter Pan*, that she would not notice the empty couch in the dark corner of the living room when she came home late in the evening.

Goldie packed up some food and a canteen of water in Robbie's invisible backpack. They had been impressed when Robbie showed it to them, but it wasn't the first magic thing they had encountered in the Land of Legends. Gretel added candy to sustain them for the long trek to the Forest of Money. Even thought it would be dark in a little while, Robbie wanted to set out immediately. There wasn't much room in the cabin and the others agreed it would be nice to sleep under the stars. As they walked, Gretel told Robbie that she had never been far from Fairy Tale Town. She was brimming with excitement and had no trouble keeping up with the older kids.

They crossed back over the yellow brick road as darkness fell. Goldie spread a large blanket and prepared to sleep under the stars. As they settled onto the blanket, a soft rain started to fall. The children snuggled close together and hoped it was just a passing sprinkle.

Robbie got out his crayon and started to draw a tarp. Without the sun, he could not see the glimmering particles of the crayon so he reached out his left hand to act as a guide while the right one drew the tarp. Surprisingly, his left hand could not feel the lines of the tarp. He felt around frantically, but found nothing. There was no tarp, there was nothing but air.

Robbie tried to think this through. *Always before, there were glittering flecks of crayon in the sunlight and I could feel the shape of whatever object I drew. Well, except for this last time when I couldn't find the invisible door. Did that mean the crayon didn't work in this world?* Robbie felt for his backpack. It was real. *So his crayon did work in this world.* He lay down on the blanket. This was puzzling. *Had his crayon stopped working?* Robbie fell asleep trying to figure this out. It had been a very long day.

Robbie woke up to see the sun peeking over the horizon, literally the crack of dawn. He was confused, but as he looked at the four other young people nestled together on the blanket, his memory returned to him. He remembered who these new friends of his were, where he was and how he came to be here. He also remembered that he had something to do so he could get back home, hopefully tonight. He quickly woke everyone so they could continue on their journey. Little Gretel bounced up ready to get going, while Hansel sat up slowly, stretched and consulted a pocket almanac he carried in his back pocket. In the morning light, Goldilocks hair shone like the gold she was named for, as she got up and started digging in the bag for some breakfast food. Then there was Blue. Robbie nudged him again with his foot as Blue laid there still as a stone on the blue side of the blanket, snoring.

Hansel took over. With two fingers, he clamped Blue's nose shut. Blue woke up with a start, in the middle of his next snore.

During the long trek to this mythical forest of money, Robbie learned a lot about his four new friends. They talked for miles about the Three Bears and all the time that Goldilocks spent babysitting Little Bear and hanging around the cottage, the numerous times that Hansel and Gretel were caught by the witch as well as the many times, like yesterday, when they visited her house while she was away. Blue and Hansel laughed about the times they snuck off to the farmer's watering hole when Blue was supposed to be watching the cows.

Robbie loved hearing the stories. He had never before had friends he could tell stories about. Sure, he was a likeable guy and the kids at school sat next to him and talked to him, but his mother worked hard to keep her life private so Robbie never had any friends over. When he was younger, he went on play dates to other kid's houses, or to the park, but when he got older, he realized he wasn't like the other kids at Hudley School. They had cell phones and computers and gaming systems. They played sports on travelling club teams. His mom couldn't afford all that, so he had learned to take comfort in his art. It wasn't a bad life.

The other four were so engrossed in their conversations they failed to notice Robbie had dropped back and was intently observing his new friends. He decided Goldilocks was the nurturer of the group, the mother hen. Blue was not only eager for adventure, but also a very smooth talker who seemed to always be in a good mood. Rather than being the young tag-along sister, little Gretel seemed to be a head strong, impulsive child. The wiser and more cautious older brother Hansel would tag-along after her to protect her, protecting her mostly from herself. Robbie wondered how he fit into this group. He had always been a loner who spent his time observing and drawing life not jumping into action and adventure. How ironic that he ended up in this crazy land where he was forced to go on an adventure or be forever separated from all that was known and loved. How lucky he was to have met up with new friends that welcomed him and his adventures for their own.

The five friends had just entered another forest when Robbie noticed a little girl walking through the woods a bit off to his left. "Hey," he yelled, "Isn't that Little Red Ri..."

Robbie couldn't finish his sentence as Blue quickly clamped his hand over Robbie's mouth. At the same time, all of the others fell silent and looked at Robbie with concern. Hansel quickly spied a large tree and pointed for Robbie to climb up it. Robbie didn't move. Goldie pushed Robbie toward the tree as Gretel ran to Hansel who boosted her up into the tree. She turned back and gestured for Robbie to follow. Hansel boosted Robbie up into the tree after Gretel, and Robbie followed Gretel into the higher branches.

"What's going on?" he whispered.

Gretel pointed to Little Red Riding Hood then searched intently through the woods below them. Finally spotting what she was seeking from this bird's eye view, she pointed it out to Robbie. A wolf was stealthily approaching though he was still quite a distance away from Little Red Riding Hood. Gretel said, "Whenever you see Red in the Deep Dark Woods, you know the wolf is not far behind."

Robbie looked worriedly at his three friends below. Hansel had boosted Goldie into the tree too, but she was having a hard time climbing it wearing a dress. She remained on the lower branches with her dress tucked around her.

Blue and Hansel ran away from the tree and started joking and talking loudly trying to attract the wolf. The wolf's ears perked up and he ran after the boys, sniffing as he ran. As the wolf neared the boys, Blue boosted Hansel into the tree. Robbie had only a moment to worry how

Blue would get into the tree before he saw Blue jump up high, grab the lowest tree branch and skillfully swing his body up into the tree like an acrobat. He didn't try to climb very high but leaned down and sneered at the Big Bad Wolf as he neared the tree.

The wolf jumped at the tree and tried to climb it, but his sharp nails wouldn't hold him and he slid down the trunk. The wolf circled the trunk and leaped at Blue a few times but could not get high enough. Blue moved up higher in the tree and Hansel took his place holding a fistful of acorns. He placed an acorn in his rolled up almanac, held it to his mouth and shot it out with a mighty blow aimed right at the rear end of the wolf. *Direct hit!* The wolf yelped. Two more acorns had the wolf backing away from the tree. Another direct hit and the wolf was running away. Hansel shot out the rest of the acorns, most of them missing as the wolf took off into the woods in the same direction Red Riding Hood had gone.

The children scrambled down out of the tree, Blue whooping and cheering about Hansel's good aim, but Robbie was worried about Red Riding Hood. "Shouldn't you try to save her from the wolf?" he asked.

Blue shook his head as he answered, "You still don't get it. This is her destiny in the LOL. She will always be chased by a wolf, and she will always survive. She can't die here. None of us can die here."

"So if you can't die, why did you all scramble up a tree?" Robbie asked.

Blue met Goldilocks' eyes and she gave him a slight nod. Blue took a deep breath and said, "We are not in danger of dying in this land, but you are. This is not your destiny. You don't yet know your destiny so we will do our best to protect you. Hansel and I had to distract the wolf from finding you, then drive him away with the acorns."

"My destiny? That sounds serious. Do you know my destiny?"

"Of course not. It is not predictable like ours," said Blue.

Robbie was silent and thoughtful. It was not difficult to accept that he could die, either here or in his own world. What was hard to accept was that these new friends of his, these wonderful new friends, were not like him at all. They looked like teenagers, except little Gretel, just like himself, but they weren't. They were centuries old. That was just too huge a concept to wrap his brain around.

Mistaking his silence for fear, Goldilocks put her hand on Robbie's back and said, "Don't worry. We will keep you safe."

Robbie gave her a weak smile and said, "Thanks."

The tired group of travelers stopped when they came to a riverbank. "Oh no!" said Hansel, "we're stuck here!"

Robbie was confused. "Why don't we just take the bridge?" he asked, pointing to the massive structure that stretched across the water.

Goldie sighed. "It's the wrong time. London Bridge is falling down," she quoted from the familiar nursery rhyme. From the looks of the scaffold by that missing span, it would be a few days before it was all built up again.

"How can this be London Bridge? We're not in London. We're not even near a city. We're not near anything," Robbie whined in frustration.

"That's just what this bridge is called and it is always falling down, then it gets all built up again," Goldie answered.

The five kids sat down on the riverbank to think. Robbie did what he liked to do whenever he needed a new idea; he took a piece of paper and pastels from his art case and started drawing. He drew his friends on the riverbank. He drew London Bridge in the background. Just for fun, he added a little boat floating under the bridge.

Robbie's friends stared at him in amazement as he quickly drew a very detailed drawing. Blue was most impressed by the array of colors and the blends that Robbie could make with his pastels. He picked it up to get a closer look. "Oops!" he said as the picture turned multiple shades of blue.

Robbie laughed at him as he held out his hand for the picture. "It looks pretty cool in all those shades of blue." As the real colors returned to the page, Robbie found himself focusing on the little boat under the bridge. He got an idea.

Robbie took out his glitter crayon and started to draw a boat. Remembering his failure from the night before, Robbie felt for the boat as he drew. Not only could he feel this boat, the sunlight was catching the glitter flecks of the crayon, so Robbie could also see the boat as he drew.

The other four stared in wonder as Robbie drew lines in the air. Blue had watched him draw with his crayon before, but even he was fascinated.

Almost as quickly as Robbie had drawn his detailed picture, he finished the boat and turned to his friends and asked, "Ready?"

Only Gretel was brave enough to speak up as she asked, "Ready for what? What did you draw?"

"It's a boat. A simple one, but let's see if it floats. Now come on, help me get it into the water."

The friends approached eagerly holding out their hands searching for the invisible boat. "I feel it!" Blue said excitedly as his hands rapidly moved over the sides and bottom of the boat. Each spot he touched sparkled a barely visible iridescent blue and illuminated the boat one section at a time. This brought wide grins to the faces of the others who then grabbed the sides of the boat.

Gretel hopped inside to test it with her feet and yelled, "Come on! Let's get it in the water and go!" Even with Gretel inside, everyone was surprised to find out just how light an invisible boat was.

Hansel asked cautiously, "How do you know this will float? How will we steer this? Will we all fit?"

Robbie handed Hansel the two oars he had just drawn and said, "There is only one way to find out."

Goldie was reluctant to climb into the boat the others were pushing into the water.

"What's wrong?" Robbie asked.

"I don't know about this," she said. "It seems dangerous. The water gets pretty rough in the middle of the river. You do know how to swim don't you?"

Robbie paled a little as he answered, "Um, well, no." After all, he had grown up in a city. Nobody swam in the polluted Beflin Bay. His mother couldn't afford to send him to the clubs with the private pools.

"You don't know how to swim and you're willing to jump into an invisible boat to cross a river you've never even seen before? Are you crazy?" Goldie said in a voice that reflected anger, as much as concern that he would do something so risky.

"You're right, it is risky," Robbie said not backing down from the decision he made. "What choice do I have? I did not ask to get stuck here, I did not want to be chased by a wolf and I do not want to paddle across a river, but I want to get home and if this is how I have to do it, then I will." Robbie turned away from her.

The other two boys were already deciding their places inside the boat. Come to think of it, they looked pretty silly climbing into an invisible boat. It reminded him of the play *Our Town* he had seen once with his mother where all of the scenery and the props were invisible. The actors and actresses were pantomiming all of their actions. He cracked a smile in spite of his situation.

Blue was now in the back of the boat with his hand bent around an invisible oar and Hansel was seated in the front, also holding an oar. "It floats!" Gretel announced from the middle of the boat.

Blue had been listening to Goldie and Robbie argue. "Look," he said. "Hansel is a really strong swimmer, if you can make a rope, we'll tie one end on you and the other end on Hansel. It's only going to take 20 minutes to row across this river. If the boat tips, Hansel will tow you into shore. Believe me, he has had lots of practice rescuing Gretel."

Hansel was nodding his head in agreement. "It's true. Gretel wanted to learn to swim so badly she would just jump in every time she was near water. Fortunately, she learned to swim after the dozenth time or so, because I don't think I could have kept up with her much longer." At

Robbie's confused expression, Hansel reassured him, "She wasn't going to drown, but she couldn't get out by herself either."

"Okay, then that will have to do," he said and quickly drew a rope and linked himself to Hansel. Robbie arranged himself with the girls in the middle, and Blue shoved the boat off into the river.

The children relaxed when they saw that this rowboat seemed as sturdy as any boat they had actually "seen". Robbie even started to enjoy himself as Blue broke into song. "Row, row, row your boat, gently down the stream." Robbie and Gretel joined in one verse later, turning the song into a round.

About halfway across the river, the wind started blowing and the current picked up speed. The joyful mood disappeared as Blue and Hansel had to row against a mounting wind just to keep the boat on course. Dark clouds rolled in. The children were almost to the other side of the river when the wind got even stronger and a hard rain started falling, as if a cloud had burst. The boys rowed frantically for the shoreline. The boat tossed in the current and Robbie held onto the side of the boat, white-knuckled. The shoreline got closer, and the water got very shallow. Goldie, who was sitting closest to the front near Hansel, hopped out with him to pull the boat up on the shore.

Blue jumped in to help. As he reached the front of the boat, a huge bolt of lightning struck along with an ear-splitting roll of thunder. Everyone jumped. The boat lurched and knocked Hansel and Goldie onto their backsides in the shallow water, causing them to lose their hold on the boat. Blue reached for the boat but grasped air instead of the invisible boat. That moment was just enough for the current to shift the boat downstream. The dark clouds prevented them from seeing the glittering outline of the boat. Gretel and Robbie were floating further away from the shore. Before Hansel had regained his footing, the rope around his waist tightened and he was being dragged downstream behind the boat fighting to stay afloat in the strong current.

Gretel and Robbie sat helpless in the boat, tossed about by the current and the wind. Robbie could feel the rope tighten around his waist, but he could not see anything through the heavy rain beating down on his head and filling his eyes with water. He was worried about Hansel, and started pulling on his rope to try and reel him in. He was peering over the side of the boat searching the choppy water for Hansel when the back of the boat struck a massive boulder jarring the boat so hard that Robbie toppled over the side. Gretel saw Robbie go under the water and without a thought for her own safety, she jumped overboard and grabbed Robbie. Tucking her arm around his neck, she yelled at him to relax then kicked with all her might toward the shoreline. Her only thought was to save Robbie as her body instinctively copied the rescue moves her brother had used on her many times. She was kicking as hard as she could, and Robbie, who was paralyzed with fear, was being towed in. Gretel got very tired and was afraid her strength would give out when she slowly realized Robbie was getting easier to drag. She spared a glance and saw Hansel, swimming hard toward the shoreline, the rope helping to pull Robbie toward the shore.

The rain lessened and Robbie was recovering from his initial shock when he saw Hansel stand up in the waist deep water. He felt Gretel's hold on him weaken, then she let go as he struggled to get his feet under him. *Land! He had made it.* He started walking toward the shore turning to take Gretel's hand. Gretel was not standing, but was floating in the water a few steps behind him. He waited for her to get her feet under her, but she didn't seem to be moving. He took a step back and grabbed her, but again she made no move to stand up. With his feet braced under him, he flipped her onto her back then dragged her unconscious form to the shore.

Hansel reached them as Robbie was pulling the limp little girl out of the water. Hansel scooped her up and carried her to the dry shore where Goldie and Blue were running to meet them. They turned her on her side as she began coughing up water.

Robbie collapsed on the shore beside Gretel.

The cloudburst passed and the rain subsided. Blue went to gather some firewood so they could dry out. When Robbie regained his strength enough to get up, his first thought was for his art case, which was not in its customary place in his hand. An overwhelming feeling of sadness overcame him as he realized the river had taken his most treasured item.

Sad as he was, he checked on Gretel. She was sitting up now as well and he thanked her for saving his life. "Um, thanks for rescuing me.

"I'm confused," Robbie said, "I thought you couldn't die?"

"Even if I can't drown, near-drownings are a bit exhausting." She leaned against him as he sat down.

Blue joined the group with an armload of firewood and a twinkle in his eye. "I found this wood along the shore. Some of it is still dry, but I'm afraid this piece is far too wet to make good firewood," he said as he held up a piece of carved wood by its ivory handle.

Robbie was on his feet in an instant, pounding Blue on the back as he claimed his beloved art case!

Goldie prepared a small lunch from the backpack she had fortuitously slipped on her back while Robbie was drawing the boat. Blue managed to get a little fire going by skillfully rubbing two sticks together. Hansel was still sitting by Gretel and hadn't said anything since bringing his sister to the shore.

Goldie tried to comfort him. She said, "Look at her. Gretel's going to be fine."

Hansel said in a serious tone, "Why did she lose consciousness? I thought for a moment she wasn't going to recover from all the water she swallowed. It's never been like this before, even before she could swim when she bobbed in the water for over an hour back at the old swimming hole. What's going on?

"Gretel and I have never been this far from Fairy Tale Town. Do you think we are still immortal out here?" Hansel asked the others.

Nobody had an answer. Only Blue had been this far from home before, and he hadn't suffered any injuries. He reached out and grabbed the end of a stick from the fire. He touched the red-hot end to his bare shin. "Yeoowwch!!" he screamed as he tossed the stick back in the fire.

Still, there was no burn mark on his leg when he brushed away the ash.

7

THE TREASURE ROOM

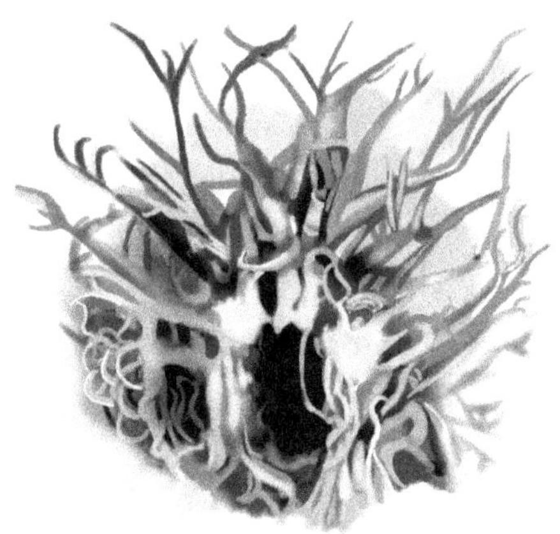

Not much further now," Blue said as they headed into a lush green valley toward a forest of trees.

"So, what is this money forest like? How much money can we pick?" Robbie was thinking he'd like to take some back to his mother.

"That's up to Elyrise the Wise," said Gretel. "He's the tender of the forest."

"So, what's Elyrise like?" asked Robbie.

"Uh..." Gretel stammered.

"Well?" pressed Robbie. When Gretel made no attempt to answer, he looked at Hansel. He shrugged his shoulders, "I told you we've never been this far from Fairy Tale Town." Robbie turned to Goldie who shook her head. He then glared at Blue who held up his hands in a helpless gesture.

"None of you have met him?" Robbie demanded.

"Why don't we just find out what he is like for ourselves," Blue suggested unconcerned, as he pointed toward a huge cave-like structure. The mouth of the "cave" was roughly circular and huge, nearly 16 feet tall. It was not set in a mountain, but appeared to be jutting out of a huge reddish-brown wall. Behind the jutting mouth of the cave, the huge wall extended in both directions. The children could see trees in the distance visible above the wall.

The five of them slowly approached the entrance of the cave wondering how they would find Elyrise the Wise. Lace designs dangled all around the mouth of the cave resembling the roots of a tree. This cave was not made of stone like other caves. It was made of wood, reddish brown wood on both the inside and out. The outside of the jutting mouth had a pattern to it. The pattern looked like bark.

"This is made to look like a tree. That's fantastic!" said Gretel.

"Except trees are not this big," Goldie responded.

"There are some giant trees called Redwood Trees that grow in Sequoia National Forest in a place called California in the western United States," reported Hansel like an Encyclopedia.

"I guess this could be a real tree that fell over, and now we're walking inside it," Blue's voice sounded deeper inside the tree.

Just then a woman glided in. She was very beautiful, and the tallest woman Robbie had ever seen. She must have been seven feet tall and had long skinny arms and legs like tree limbs. Her brown hair sparkled with colorful leaves that decorated it. When she smiled at the five visitors, it felt like the room brightened. "Hello, I'm Elyrison, daughter of Elyrise the Wise, tender of the trees. My two sisters and I are wood nymphs and we live among the trees, nurturing them and planting seedlings. Welcome to our forest. You must have had a long walk. Can I get you something to drink? Our specialty drink is sassafras tea. We also have iced sassafras tea or sassafras flavored snow cones."

The children stared as she managed to get all of that out without taking a second breath. They all nodded their heads appreciatively even though they had no idea what they were agreeing to.

"Wonderful. I'll ring for my sister Elyrisia. She makes it the best. Meanwhile, I will show you to our visitors' room. Follow me." She did not slow her talking down as she started leading the way into the artificially lit and very spacious hallway. "You can make yourselves comfortable and rest after that weary walk. I know the nearest road is quite a distance from here where London Bridge crosses the water. The Bridge is out, so we haven't had anyone from Fairy Tale Town in quite a while." Her gaze rested on Hansel and Gretel who were so easily recognizable in their German outfits. "I don't know how you crossed the river, but I do know that nobody makes that walk unless they really need to come here. Of course, you must be here to see my father about picking some money. Elyrise the Wise is tending to some of the older trees that just got struck in a thunderstorm earlier today...." With that she paused and raised her long wispy eyebrows as she searched their faces.

"You must have been caught in that thunderstorm too. Wow! It was a doozey! I hope you are unharmed, but of course you are. I can see all of you are in one piece even if you do look a little roughed up." This time, Elyrison's gaze fell on Robbie, but she did not wait for him to answer. "Here we are, go on in and rest. Refreshments are on the way!" With that, she turned and whisked away like a light branch on a windy day.

The group was left staring after her, momentarily speechless.

"Well," Robbie said. "Elyrison seemed nice."

"Like a gust of wind," Goldie remarked.

"A bit long-winded," muttered Hansel.

"I guess we just make ourselves comfortable while we wait," Goldie said and found a comfortable place to sit as her hostess had suggested. It was an overstuffed loveseat with an embroidered cover that was very inviting. Gretel curled up next to her looking tired after the long and challenging journey. Hansel chose a straight-backed metal chair. A chair that resembled a throne captured Robbie's interest. He studied its velvet cover and jewel studded arms and back.

"You don't think these are real gems, do you?" he asked the others.

"They look like rubies, emeralds, sapphires and diamonds to me. Are they cold to the touch?" asked Hansel.

Robbie gently ran his fingers over the stones, which were indeed cool to his touch.

Hansel was studying his metal chair. "Um guys, do you think this chair is real silver?"

Goldie studied her loveseat. It was embroidered with a beautiful intricate silk pattern.

When they looked to see what treasure Blue was sitting on, they realized he wasn't with them.

"LBB, where are you?" Hansel called out.

"I'm back here," Blue yelled excitedly. "You guys have got to see this!"

Gretel perked up and bounced out of her seat to go to Blue, her fatigue forgotten for the moment. Hansel was right on her heels as he called out, "Wait for me young lady. You don't know anything about this place. We must be careful."

Robbie and Goldie decided to join the others as well.

Blue had wandered behind the chairs to a room that appeared to go on as far as the eye could see, though the passageway got narrower and narrower just like a limb of a tree moving away from the trunk. The room was cluttered with furniture, statues, paintings and tapestries all over the smooth wood walls. Gretel spotted a nearby cherry cabinet whose doors had designs of ivory inlaid on the panels. She pulled open the doors and a dozen necklaces hung from the hooks inside the cabinet. The necklaces were priceless--pearls, diamonds, gems of every sort. She especially loved the simple necklace with the amethyst pendant since purple was her favorite color.

Hansel was watching her and warned, "Don't touch anything! It's not ours."

But Gretel was already holding the amethyst up to her neck as she peered in a mirror with beautiful etchings of faeries along its edges. "I know. I just want to see what it looks like." She glanced once more at her image then carefully put it back into the cabinet and closed the doors.

Hansel wandered over to a large wooden bookcase that was overflowing with leather bound classic books with gold lettering on the cover.

Goldilocks was staring at a tapestry of a Victorian lady in a stunning ball gown standing in a gazebo draped with flowers. Goldie was impressed by the tiny stitches that someone had taken the time to hand sew.

Robbie was oblivious to the others as he studied the paintings. Some were landscapes, some were still life, some were portraits, while still others were abstract expressions of art. All of them were impressive. Many of these pieces were created by talented artists he recognized from his world. He saw works by the masters including Rembrandt, Monet, Picasso, and Michelangelo. He wondered if this was where "lost masterpieces" ended up. Robbie was attracted to the bold color choices used by Picasso, as well as the more subtle watercolors used by Monet. He chuckled to himself when he saw some of the art from the Blue Period, and shared a laugh with Blue when he called him over to see them.

Having studied a lot of Art History in his school library, Robbie recognized much of the art signed by the Masters, but unfamiliar artists signed some of the art as well. He was drawn to a particular landscape painting done in pastels by an artist known as *pierres,* signed in all lower case. The artist had blended colors to achieve the most beautiful shades. The mountains in the picture were shaped like a sleeping giant in various shades of brown: sepia, mahogany, caramel, chestnut and sienna. At the giant's feet, flowed a waterfall through a divided peak. The trees on the mountains were gorgeous blends of green: sage, apple green, hunter green, forest green and olive interwoven in a rich spectrum of color that made it appear vibrant and alive. The azure blue sky was so realistic with its puffy white clouds that Robbie wanted to fly into it.

The incredible blue green foaming water of the waterfall cascaded and splashed with life. Robbie was mesmerized by the way the artist had created shafts of sunlight whose rays just touched the mountaintops, reflected in the spray flowing over the fall and the ripples in the pool at the base of the falls.

Robbie lost himself in the painting and had no idea how much time had passed when he heard a deep voice behind him.

"Beautiful, isn't it? It's one of my favorites. I'm very fond of the blend of colors the artist achieved," said the voice as if it was reading Robbie's thoughts.

Robbie turned to see the face of an old man with white hair who was nearly eight feet tall. The wrinkles of his face resembled tree bark, but his eyes sparkled with kindness. He was dressed in long robes that shimmered an iridescent green like the color of leaves in sunlight.

"Hello. I am Elyrise. I understand your group has come to see me," the tall old man said.

"Yes," Robbie said, then remembered his manners and held out his hand. "It's nice to meet you. My name is Robbie Sartes and I'm here with my friends Little Boy Blue, Goldilocks and Hansel and Gretel from Fairy Tale Town."

Elyrise was mesmerized for a moment as he stared into Robbie's lavender eyes. Then, he recovered as he shook Robbie's hand and nodded his head at the others who had gathered around to meet him.

"I see Elyrison has shown you to my treasure room, while Elyria has delivered Elyrisia's refreshments to the tea room. Shall we go?" Elyrise gestured to the door through which they had entered. They crossed the main hall, which they now recognized as the trunk of a fallen tree into another narrow passageway, or branch, of this home, making a left into yet a smaller passageway resembling a cozy sitting room.

"Please allow me to freshen up while you enjoy your refreshments," requested Elyrise as he guided them into the room then turned to walk quickly away. As he turned, Robbie noticed one side of his clothes were wet and smudged with mud.

The site of Elyrise's stately figure had all but taken their breath away as they looked at each other in awe. Only then did they notice that Gretel was missing!

"Hansel, where is Gretel?" Goldie asked in concern.

"I don't know. I was so stunned by Elyrise the Wise I didn't notice her," he admitted ashamedly as he hurried back into the main hall.

"Don't blame yourself, I don't remember if she met Elyrise either," Goldie said sympathetically, and the other two boys shook their heads.

"Maybe she stopped to look at something and couldn't figure out where the rest of us had gone," Robbie spoke up as he noticed how many passageways there were leading off the main hall.

"Let's split up so we can find her faster," said Blue. "Goldie, you wait with the refreshments in case any of our hosts return and you can ask for their help. Anybody, got any breadcrumbs so we don't get lost?"

Hansel paled, then realized Blue was just trying to lighten the mood.

Robbie dug into his backpack and gave each of the boys a handful of gold pebbles.

"Meet back here in a few minutes," Blue called back as he headed down a nearby passage.

Each of the boys took off in a different direction and Robbie headed back to the treasure room. He called to Gretel, but there was no answer. With so many amazing things, a little girl might easily get lost in here, especially a curious and fearless little girl. He returned to the back of the room, drawn once again to the beautiful paintings. He stole one more glance at the colorful landscape with the mountains and the waterfall and the tiny cabin drawn off to the side.

He called out to Gretel again as he quickly explored the huge room. Then he noticed the cherry cabinet she had opened earlier, and he saw that she had left the door slightly open. He stepped over to close it and was surprised to see the angelic face of little Gretel curled up inside the cabinet fast asleep. He opened both doors to lift the sleeping child and noticed that one of her feet was not visible. Her ankle seemed to disappear at the back of the cabinet. His hand also vanished when he reached back to retrieve her foot. What should have been the back of the cabinet was just opaque air. Remembering the door that led him into the Land of Legends, Robbie leaned his head over the sleeping child and poked it through the barrier. What he saw made him shudder and withdraw quickly.

His sudden movement in the cramped space woke Gretel. "Come on," he said as he patted her gently, "the others are worried about you."

As he led Gretel from the room, he asked, "Did you happen to notice anything unusual in the back of that cabinet?"

She answered sleepily, "There was a fur coat on the bottom that made a really soft, comfortable cushion inside the cabinet."

Robbie decided to forget it for now. He did not need further adventure. He returned to the room with the refreshments where the others were just gathering. Everyone hugged Gretel who apologized and said, "Sorry I guess I was tired and fell asleep."

The boys handed the golden pebbles back to Robbie, which they had collected on their return from their searches, not wanting to upset Elyrise by littering his home.

They sat down on the couches in front of an oblong coffee table whose sides were rough and uneven resembling the cross-section of a tree trunk, only the rings were of various colors. It felt more like marble than wood.

"Do you like it?" Elyrise the Wise asked Robbie, as the stately figure returned to the room. If he noticed that the group had not started eating yet, he was too polite to say anything. "It's a piece of petrified wood from a very large tree."

Robbie agreed that it was impressive and took a taste of his half-melted snow shake. Sassafras is a unique flavor, he decided, but after two or three more mouthfuls, he decided he liked it. His friends were eating their snow shakes with equal pleasure.

Elyrise noticed Gretel and asked warmly, "Who do we have here?"

Hansel quickly introduced his sister and gave a brief account of their recent search and recover mission.

Elyrise laughed richly when he heard that Gretel had fallen asleep in the cabinet then sat down next to her on the couch and asked, "So, what brings you youngsters to my forest?"

The five friends looked at one another, but no one said a word.

"Let me make this easier for you. How much money did you hope to pick from my trees?" asked Elyrise with a twinkle in his eye.

Blue spoke up, "He needs one thousand dollars to get a..."

"Yes, Mr. Elyrise sir" Robbie interrupted before Blue could tell him his whole life story. "I know it's a lot to ask, but I do need one thousand dollars, and I am afraid I will not be able to pay you back for it."

8

THE TEST

Would you like a tour of my forest?" asked Elyrise the Wise after the children had finished every bit of the sassafras shakes and pastries that Elyrisia had made and Elyria had delivered. Elyria looked very much like Elyrison, but with white blond hair. Despite their appearance, their personalities were vastly different. Elyria spoke no words as she brought the children refills of pastries with a shy smile on her face.

Gretel hopped out of her seat, recharged from her catnap, and was standing at Elyrise the Wise's chair in an instant. "Yes sir, please sir. Can we see your forest now? Please sir!"

Elyrise patted her on the head like an adoring grandfather. He held out his hand to lead her to the forest as the others fell in line.

"These are our young saplings, all in their first year of life," explained Elyrise. Outside in the forest, the children walked past row after row of young trees. These had few leaves and no money growing on them.

"This next set of trees is also very young, between one and four years old," Elyrise said gesturing toward the next dozen rows.

"Look! I see it. There is money growing on it," Blue said as he looked at the tree closest to him. There were a few dollar bills hanging from the branches next to leaves. Other leaves looked like normal leaves on one end, but the bottoms of the leaves were squared off and streaked with color. The leaves turned into dollar bills as they grew and matured. The children spent the next few minutes running from tree to tree looking at the dollar bills hanging from them.

Elyrise the Wise was pleased at the enthusiasm of the youth. In a loud voice that caught the attention of the five friends, he said, "If you wish to continue the tour, you can follow me this way."

The trees got taller as they continued down the path into the forest. "These trees here are between five and nine years old." Elyrise gestured to the next dozen rows of trees.

Robbie noticed something different about these trees in addition to their increased height, the dollars hanging from the branches were five-dollar bills. Amazing! Not only did money grow on trees in this enchanted forest, but it came in different denominations. He had little time to wonder whether the money grew in just ones and fives as Elyrise was quickly making strides past this section of the forest.

"Now, these trees here are at least ten years old," explained Elyrise.

Robbie looked at these branches. There were fewer new leaves and mostly fully developed dollar bills. Ten-dollar bills!

Blue noticed the same thing and asked Elyrise, "Do you have any twenty-year-old trees?"

"If you'll come this way," Elyrise said. After striding past two dozen more rows, Elyrise pointed to trees as tall as two-story houses.

Just as Blue expected, there were twenties growing on these trees. Of course, he could only see the denominations on the lower branches of these tall trees.

Gretel twirled around in a circle with arms outstretched and saw trees in every direction as far as her eyes could see. Now, everyone was sticking close together so they wouldn't get lost in this more mature, dense forest.

"Mr. Elyrise, Sir. Just how old are the oldest trees in your forest?" asked Robbie trying for tact.

"I have been tending this forest for over 100 years. Some of the trees in this forest have been here longer than I," explained Elyrise nodding further up the path.

Gretel tugged on the sleeve of Elyrise the Wise. His eyes twinkled when he looked down at this adorable little girl. "Please sir, may we pick some money so Robbie can give it to the Wizard and be able to go home?"

Elyrise's ears perked up at the mention of the Wizard. "You have been to see the Wizard? You must tell me all about your visit over dinner. Elyrisia has been preparing a feast for you since you first arrived. She's quite partial to children, and we don't get many visitors." He asked, "You are hungry, aren't you?"

The five friends were indeed very hungry despite the pastries from before the tour, and Robbie for one hadn't had a hot meal since eating the porridge at the Three Bear's house. *Oh yeah*, he remembered, *even his porridge had been a cold meal.*

For whatever reason, Elyrise wasn't inviting them to start taking money from the trees, so they turned their thoughts to food for the time being.

Dinner was quite an event in Elyrise the Wise's huge tree turned house. The guests were shown to a very large dining room with a table that could seat twenty people. To indicate that this was more of a family style dinner than a formal dinner party, the guests were seated together with their hosts at one end of the long banquet table. Elyrise, of course, sat at the head of the table. The three daughters joined him after serving platters of pork, chicken, steak, mashed potatoes, corn on the cob, baked beans, fresh fruit salad, macaroni and cheese and apple sauce.

They had already met the outgoing Elyrison and the very quiet Elyria. Now, they got a chance to meet Elyrisia, the very talented chef. Elyrisia was also tall and thin and looked so much like her sisters, they could be triplets. Her hair was strawberry blond and was also decorated with ornamental leaves. Elyrisia had a warm smile, a gentle manner and a kind way of speaking that showed she was very fond of children. Of the three daughters, she seemed the most like her father.

Initially, Elyrison kept up a constant stream of chatter. "I'm sorry I left you in the treasure room instead of the tea room. I hope you weren't too uncomfortable in there waiting for your refreshments?" She didn't wait for an answer, but continued speaking in her non-stop monologue. "Did you enjoy your tour of the money trees? Of course, you did. Nowhere else in the world can you find such a thing. I just love it. Did father tell you how we plant new seedlings every year? He's usually too humble to mention how much work goes into the planting and tending of the trees. Did you know that there are no seasons in the Forest of Money and very few of the 'leaves' ever fall to the ground? Well of course you didn't know that."

The children were amazed that Elyrison could say so much so quickly and in one breath. They were so dumbfounded they could merely nod or shake their heads unable to get in a word of conversation as she continued to ramble. It wasn't as if Elyrison ever waited for a reply. In fact, hungry as they were for this delicious food, they had yet to put in their first mouthful as they continued to stare while Elyrison talked.

"How is the food? I hope there is something you like to eat. Elyrisia made all of the things she thought children most enjoyed eating. Wait until you see the desserts. I told her that all of you would probably be happy to skip dinner and go right for the desserts, but she insisted you needed to eat healthy to keep up your strength and to avoid getting a tummy ache. Save room for the chocolate cake, apple pie and pudding. Am I forgetting anything dear?" Elyrison turned to Elyrisia for the answer to this last question.

Although there was barely a pause, Elyrsia said, "Don't forget the chocolate chip cookies."

"Oh yes, and chocolate chip cookies," continued Elyrison. "Those are father's particular favorite. I'm sure you will find something to your liking. She is such a gale in the kitchen. We try to help her, but most of the time, we are just in her way. She is hoping that you will stay with us for a few days. What do you think?"

"Well, uh." Even the smooth-talking Blue was at a loss for words.

"Elyrison, I think you are overwhelming the poor dears. Why don't we stop asking them questions and allow them to eat while their food is still hot," Elyrisia said in an attempt to rescue the five guests.

"Yes, Elyrison, you should take some time to eat as well," said her father, reaching out to pat her hand affectionately.

It was a very pleasant dinner with plenty of conversation, good food, and friendly company. Robbie thought this must be what it feels like to eat dinner every night with a large family. He wouldn't know. When his mother was in a play, he usually grabbed his own meals. He was an expert at making scrambled eggs, canned soup or macaroni and cheese. He could heat up any frozen food that came with directions on the box. When his mother was between plays, she did cook for them, but dinners were just the two of them, unless they were invited to Rosalie's house. Thinking about his mother made him a little homesick. He missed her stories about the crazy lives of the actors and actresses she had met in show-biz before her accident. Some had run away from home at 16 to try to make it big. Some had married four times. Some had crazy diets, crazy exercise routines, and crazy rituals. One Diva even smeared mayonnaise on her entire body and wrapped herself in plastic wrap before bed every night to preserve her youthful looks and keep away the wrinkles. All in all, his mother was a lot of fun. Since she had difficulty remembering new things that happened to her, she relied on her imagination and would invent the greatest stories to tell Robbie. He would write them down so they could act them out. Sometimes they would take walks around town and Gabrielle would make up stories about the jewelry shop owner or the librarian, whom she said were actually bad guys with secret identities. Sometimes, they would start running as fast as they could down secret alleys and into hidden gardens to hide from the imaginary villains.

Elyrise the Wise noticed Robbie staring at his plate, lost in his own thoughts. He held out a copper coin and commented, "You are very quiet my young friend. A penny for your thoughts?"

"I just have a lot on my mind, like trying to get home to my mother and my frustrating visit to the Wizard," explained Robbie.

"Ah, do tell me about the Wizard," Elyrise encouraged. "An odd man, yes, but don't underestimate his wisdom."

"I don't think he had much time to share wisdom with me. I asked to borrow a device to help me get home, and he mumbled some rhyme-thing and said it would cost me one thousand dollars. That's what brought me here."

"Can you remember the rhyme?" asked Elyrise with unmasked curiosity.

Robbie reached below the table and pulled the rhyme from his art case. Fortunately, the art case had a very tight water seal and none of its contents had gotten wet in the river. He opened his notepad and recited:

Thine eyes have I seen once with mine.
A pair of two over this time.
Over the Hew Mondz Hills, below a peak,
There you will find what most you seek.

"Hmmm, the Human's Hills you say? Is that where you are from then?" inquired Elyrise.

"No sir, I don't exactly know what or where the Human's Hills are," answered Robbie correcting the way he pronounced the unfamiliar place.

Elyrise paused for a long time with his fingers steepled below his nose. Robbie thought that if he had grandparents, he would want a grandfather just like Elyrise, or given his age, maybe a Great Grandfather. Then Elyrise spoke again in his most comforting voice. "The Human's Hills is a town to the west where humans and heroes live." Robbie waited to hear more, but that was all Elyrise was going to say about that. He then said, "I think now you should tell me where your family is from."

Robbie glanced at his friends around the table, but they were talking with the sisters who were entertained watching as everything Blue touched turned blue. All were laughing as Elyrison teased Elyrisia about the beautiful presentation of food, suggesting she should have stuck to blueberries. There was something about this meal, this family's kindness, and this man's sympathetic eyes that convinced Robbie to tell Elyrise his story.

"I'm from Rosecrest City, sir. Only I don't exactly know where that is in relation to the Land of Legends, because I never heard of the Land of Legends until yesterday. I can tell you that Rosecrest City is on planet Earth, if that means anything," explained Robbie. The old man said nothing but assessed him with his eyes. Since meeting the man, Robbie felt that Elyrise knew a lot of things, even helpful things, which Elyrise chose to keep to himself.

"All I know is that I found a magic crayon. I drew an invisible door that opened to this place, this world. Then I got distracted by a unicorn and lost track of my invisible door. That's when I met Blue, who said I could get a transparency detector from the Wizard to find my door, and you know the rest." Robbie felt somewhat relieved, explaining his situation rather than keeping secrets.

As the conversation continued further down the table, Robbie told Elyrise about his mother. Out of habit, he carefully avoided telling Elyrise about any of Gabrielle's money troubles. Instead, he explained that she was a great actress, had a terrific imagination and was a lot of fun. Even though, there were times when he didn't see much of his mother for days, this adventure was Robbie's first time away from home. Even at 13 years old, he was missing his mother tonight.

"Now son, tell me about your father," said Elyrise.

Robbie cringed out of habit when a man called him "son". It always made him feel the loss of his father even more. "There's really very little to tell you. He was gone before I was born, and my mom won't talk about him. She called him Sebastian, and said he was an artist and that this was his art box." He reached down to grab his art case that was never further than an arm's length from him.

Elyrise reached for the box. "May I?"

Robbie nodded and carefully set the box on the table in front of the kind old man. Elyrise examined the artistic lines of the lion, tracing his fingers in the grooves of the mane just like Robbie often did.

"This is a very fine box, son. As you may have noticed while in my treasure room, I am a collector of fine things. Things of beauty. Masterpieces. Do you have any idea where this box may have come from?"

"Sorry, Sir. I really know nothing more about my father or where he could have gotten this. I do know that he loved it and my mother was surprised he left it behind. She guessed he wanted to leave me something," explained Robbie.

Thump!

A sudden noise interrupted the conversations. Poor sleepy Gretel, seated between Elyrise and Elyrisia, had fallen asleep with her spoon in her hand, and her weary head landed in her chocolate pudding.

Elyrisia hurried over to clean her off with a napkin, "You poor dears, you must be exhausted. Let us show you to our guest rooms."

Robbie squirmed uncomfortably. There was just one more thing that had to be done before they could rest. So far, no one had figured out how to ask permission to pick some money from the kindly hosts' trees. The clock was ticking and Robbie was anxious to get back home.

"Excuse me, sir," Blue also knew they needed to get down to business and assumed the role of their spokesperson. "You and your daughters have been wonderful hosts. We really enjoyed the tour of this magnificent house and your legendary garden. I know you said you don't get many visitors, but those who do visit are probably interested in your money trees. We don't mean to be rude or greedy, but we also came for your money trees. If we could just pick the money, we could be on our way. Please, sir."

"Relax, my boy," said Elyrise jovially. "Of course, I remember that you wanted to pick one thousand dollars from my trees to give to the Wizard. Can you forgive an old man for wanting to spend some pleasant time with his visitors before doing business? We can talk about it tomorrow. You are tired and it is dark. Besides, even if I wanted to hurry you on your way, I'm afraid that would have to wait until morning." With that Elyrise the Wise turned and lifted a shade on the nearby wall that was covering a knothole. This section of the house looked over some of the five-year-old trees, only instead of leaves, there were crumpled paper balls visible in the moonlight.

"The leaves curl up at night," explained Elyrise as he got up to leave. "We can discuss your new mission in the morning."

"Mission?" Robbie repeated. "You mean our return trip home, I hope?"

Elyrise paused with a quizzical expression. "I assume your group knows of the test required from the one who picks the money?"

Their silence was their answer.

"Well, be that as it may, we will discuss it in more detail in the morning." Elyrise the Wise took his leave and called out to his guests to have a pleasant night's sleep.

After well wishes for a good night from Elyrisia, Elyria led the children back to the main corridor, Hansel carrying the sleeping Gretel, down another branch of the huge tree. This branch split, leading to a bedroom in each direction. Elyria pointed the girls into one room and the boys into another. A small bathroom was nestled between the bedrooms.

The shy Elyria avoided eye contact with the young people and kept her head bowed so that her white blond hair fell across her face. As she turned to go, she pointed to some fresh nightclothes and quietly asked if they needed anything else before she slipped away. “She’s like a wisp of air and Elyrisia is a gentle breeze,” Robbie poetically finished Blue’s earlier analogy.

9

THE JOURNEY CONTINUES

"What do you think he meant by a test? What kind of test?" asked Robbie. Although his grades in school were fine, they were not great. He was not exactly the studious type, spending his time with art books more than textbooks and enjoying imaginative things more than facts. "I'm afraid I'm not very good at tests," he admitted anxiously to the boys and Goldie, who had crept into the boys' room in the morning, leaving Gretel sleeping in her bed.

"Don't worry about it. I'll take it for you," said the fearless Blue who had finally woken up after a thorough shaking.

"Do you think that is a very good idea?" asked Goldie. She knew that Blue didn't spend much time at school because of his job. He was smart and had taught himself to read, write and do math, but test taking was not his strength.

"Okay, we'll let Hansel take it. He always has his nose in a book, and he's the smartest person at school," said Blue.

"How can you go to school for over a hundred years? I can't imagine four more years of high school, but for you school is unending."

"Our school is very different than yours. After we master the foundations of reading and math, we are no longer taught them at school; instead, we work on them at home for the fun of it. Our school meets only two days a week for two hours; plus, we only have school two of the four seasons each year. Instead of history, we study current events and other cultures like yours in the World Out There," Hansel explained.

"Excuse me if I sound rude, but if you know all about the world I live in, why don't you have the modern conveniences we have? A car would have made this trip a lot easier for us then a day of hiking," Robbie commented.

"As I said, we study other cultures and watch their successes and their failures. Some of the cultures we watch are older and more advanced than yours. We have witnessed cultures that were so technologically advanced, they destroyed themselves. We prefer the simple life, keeping technology to a minimum," explained Hansel.

"We do enjoy some modern conveniences." Goldie said, and pointed toward the bathroom with indoor plumbing and hot water and electric lights.

"So how exactly do you 'study' other cultures?" Robbie asked.

"Through satellites that broadcast into a station at our school. We watch things on an Omniview," explained Hansel.

"Is school the only place that has an Omniview?"

"No," Hansel answered. "Town Hall has one too, as does the theater in Fairy Tale Town. Omniviews are hard to come by and few people actually have them. Besides, we don't promote televisions in every home like your culture. It makes people lazy and less social."

"Can you zoom in on certain people? I mean, have you ever seen me? How about my mom? She's an actress—Gabrielle Sartes? She is starring in Peter Pan right now." Robbie asked excitedly.

"At school, we watch the news, and the government. The theater shows the arts, mainly new shows. The princesses don't like to see other people playing their roles, even though they need people to keep reading their stories. Sorry, I can't say I've heard your mother's name," Goldie said sympathetically. The boys remained quiet.

Elyria knocked on their door to invite them to breakfast. She knew they were anxious to be on their way. The children were grateful that it had not been Elyrison as they were not ready for her endless stream of chatter so early in the morning. Somehow, they were not surprised to find that Elyria had freshly laundered their clothes, and Elyrisia had made them a huge breakfast with sausage, pancakes, eggs, and waffles with strawberries and whipped cream on top. They quickly stuffed themselves and headed to the garden to meet Elyrise.

"Come Robbie, it's time to tell you about the test," Elyrise said to Robbie, gesturing him away from the group.

"Excuse me sir," Blue stepped up. "Would it be okay if we selected which one of us will take the test?"

"Well..." Elyrise started to answer, but Robbie interrupted.

"No, that's okay," Robbie said and looked at his friends. "I'm going to take this test. I know I don't take tests well, but this is my mission. I'm the one that needs the money. You guys have been amazing and I can't thank you enough for all of your help, but this is my test to pass or fail and I can't ask anyone else to take if for me."

"Well done, my son," Elyrise said leading Robbie off alone. "You may be happy to know that you have already passed part of this test. The first part was a test of character. You have shown impeccable character since we have met. It was no coincidence that Elyrisia led you to the treasure room when you arrived. She left you there so she could observe you from some knotholes in the wall. Neither you nor your friends attempted to steal any of the very valuable items in there. Even the little one did not keep that amethyst necklace she admired so much," Elyrise said with affection. "By accepting this challenge, you have shown determination and strength of character."

"Thank you, sir. I'll do my best with the rest of the test," Robbie said, anxious for the test to continue.

After what seemed to Robbie like a very long pause, Elyrise broke his silence with a cryptic phrase delivered in a voice as rich as mahogany and as strong as oak:

"Over the hills through the In Betweenz
You will discover what this task means
Find answers long sought out
And bring back a treasure beyond a doubt."

Without a word, Robbie took out his sketchbook and pencil and added this rhyme below the Wizard's rhyme. He remained holding the pencil over his notebook as he waited for Elyrise to continue.

Elyrise was no longer standing next to Robbie, but was walking back toward his house in the tree trunk. Robbie's friends were entertaining themselves in this vast and fascinating garden. Only Blue seemed to be paying any attention to the exchange between Robbie and the wise man. When Blue could offer Robbie no guidance, Robbie decided he was supposed to follow Elyrise, because surely there was more to this "test".

Elyrise held the door open for Robbie, and then wordlessly glided down the corridor while thoughts raced in Robbie's head. *Was the phrase some kind of riddle that he was supposed to solve? Were they headed to the In Betweenz and was that where he would be told what he was supposed to do?"*

When Elyrise stopped, Robbie who was lost in his thoughts nearly collided into the trunk of the silent old man. He recognized this part of the tree house. It was the exact spot where he had noticed all of the amazing paintings by the Masters and some very talented unknowns.

In fact, Elyrise was standing in front of the very same picture that had captivated Robbie on the previous day. It was the colorful landscape signed by *pierres*.

At last, Elyrise spoke, "This room is filled with my treasures. Treasures made by very talented people. Talent like this can't be bought with all the money in the world. When you live in a land where gold has no value, and you tend a garden where money grows on trees—you learn to value other things like talent, beauty, family, hard work, courage, and self-discovery.

"Robbie, I knew when I met you that we had something in common. You value beauty and are working hard to return to your home and family, and you are courageous to accept the challenge of my test. Money is not the most important thing to you, or you would have asked for more than one thousand dollars for the Wizard. When I saw you staring at my favorite painting yesterday, I decided we were kindred spirits. So, for your test, I'm going to ask of you something that I hold in high esteem—something else from this artist, and the joy of self-discovery as you seek what you find."

Side by side, they gazed again at the picture in front of them. Then Robbie asked if the picture had a name and where he might find the artist, *pierres*.

Instead of answering him, Elyrise held a package out to Robbie. "Now, I have given you everything you will need for this test. You will find your friends waiting for you at the entrance. Good luck, my son." With that, Elyrise turned and glided out of the room.

Robbie made a quick sketch of the beautiful painting in his notebook, trying to commit every detail to memory.

Where are you pierres?

Robbie found his friends waiting anxiously for him at the cave-like entrance of the big tree that housed Elyrise and his daughters. They were sitting at an outdoor cafe table sipping iced sassafras tea.

"What happened?" asked Blue.

"Did you pass your test?" asked Goldilocks.

"Was it hard?" asked Gretel.

"Did you get your money?" asked Hansel, "Can we go home now?"

Robbie sighed long and hard, sitting down to drink the iced sassafras tea Elyrisia had left for him. "Unfortunately, we cannot go home yet. The test was not a paper and pencil test, but a quest, and yes, it is hard. It is so hard that I have absolutely no idea what to do next."

"What happened?" asked Blue again, impatiently.

"He told me I needed to get him another painting by *pierres*, like the one hanging in the treasure room," Robbie said with another big sigh.

"Then what happened?" asked Blue.

"Then he handed me this bag and told me it contained everything I'd need."

As discouraged as Robbie was, Blue was excited by the promise of more adventure. "Remember this is Elyrise the Wise. If he said you have everything you need, then let's get started. Maybe there are more clues in the bag?"

With a glimmer of hope, Robbie peered into the half full sack, roughly the size of a pillowcase. When he emerged, Robbie said, "It's food."

"And?" asked Blue expectantly.

"Just food and this," said Robbie holding up a little brown change purse. He opened the change purse to find exactly fifty dollars. "That's everything," he said after checking for any hidden items in the sack, "Except for these garlic bulbs". He crinkled his nose at those and returned them to the sack.

"Okay," said Blue "We know he expected you to need fifty dollars. Maybe that is the price of the painting. How much food is in the bag?"

"Enough to feed all of us for a day, maybe a little more," said Robbie.

"I bet we have to go on another day long journey to get this painting," said Blue.

"Or maybe the journey only takes half a day," Goldilocks said hopefully, "We have half the food for the way there and the other half for the way home."

"Maybe he just expects Robbie to go alone, so there's enough food to last one person several days," said Hansel who had originally come on the journey only to protect Gretel.

"Maybe," said Robbie, "but there are five peanut butter and jelly sandwiches, cookies, apples and five pieces of cold chicken which has to be eaten today or it will go bad. Besides, Elyrise did say my friends were outside waiting for me. I'm pretty sure we are supposed to travel together. The question is, where are we traveling?"

"You forgot to mention Elyrise said that about us, so exactly what *else* did Elyrise say?" demanded Hansel, "and don't leave anything out."

Robbie repeated everything he remembered from his conversation with Elyrise, reading the rhyme word for word from his notebook.

"Read the rhyme again," insisted Hansel.

So Robbie repeated,

"Over the hills through the In Betweenz
You will discover what this task means.
Find answers long sought out
And bring back a treasure beyond a doubt."

"That's it then," said Hansel.

"It is?" asked Blue.

"It is?" repeated Robbie.

"Of course. We have to climb over those hills and pass through the In Betweenz," said Hansel pointing to the hills just visible to the north.

"Let's get going then," Robbie stood up, grabbed his art case, adjusted his invisible backpack, and tried to toss the sack on his back as well.

Blue reached over and took the sack from him and Goldie cleared her throat, "Who's going to tell him why we can't just march through the In Betweenz?"

At first nobody replied, then Gretel blurted out, "Nobody is safe in the In Betweenz. That's the land between these hills and the Human's Hills. The bad guys live in the In Betweenz."

"What do you mean by 'bad guys'?" asked Robbie.

"Werewolves, vampires, the Boogeyman, and other horrible creatures." Hansel stated solemnly.

Robbie laughed, "There are no such things as werewolves, vampires, and the Boogeyman. They're just myths and leg..." but Robbie couldn't finish his sentence as he remembered that his friends were all fairy tale characters in this Land of Legends with its magical doors, King Midas, Money Trees, and apparently the Boogeyman.

"I believe you, but I have to risk it if I want to go home," said Robbie. "Besides, you already told me you can't die so what do you have to fear?"

"Mortals think that dying is the worst thing in the world, but there are some things we consider worse than death, like becoming changers or being haunted by the Boogeyman every night," explained Goldie. Fairy tales have never crossed the In Betweenz."

"What are changers?" asked Robbie.

Blue explained, "Changers are people that turn into horrible things at night, like werewolves and vampires. In theory, a Fairy Tale could still live a storybook life by day and change into a horrible creature by night. But we don't know that would happen to us, because Fairy Tales don't cross the In Betweenz."

"You're quiet Hansel. What are you thinking?" asked Goldilocks.

"I don't know, I've read a bit about the In Betweenz, but like you said, no Fairy Tale has ever ventured there. Gretel had a difficult time at our river crossing which was unexpected. I'm wondering if we become more vulnerable the further we get from home.

"You're right, then. You can't go. You stay here and wait for me, but I've got to get started," Robbie said as he grabbed the bag back from Blue, swung it over his shoulder and started heading for the hills. *I've been doing things by myself all of my life. I can do this too. Only things are different now,* he sulked. He had learned to enjoy the company of friends, and he had learned to depend on them to share the burden. A moment later, the bag was pulled out of his hands as Blue swung it over his own shoulder.

Blue punched Robbie in the arm, "What can I say? I have had more fun with you in the last two days than I can ever remember. I'm in. Besides, I may not have been to the In Betweenz, but I rode out this way on Pegasus and was just fine."

"And by Pegasus, you mean the winged horse?" asked Robbie.

"The one and only."

"Fantastic," replied Robbie.

"Wait for me," said Goldie. Then he saw Gretel breaking away from Hansel. He smiled to himself, sure that Hansel would follow Gretel, and the five of them would venture on together.

10

HORROR IN THE IN BETWEENZ

Although it took several hours, the five friends hiked through the hills leading to the In Betweenz with very few mishaps. That is, unless you count Goldie stumbling at the top of one hill and tumbling down the whole hill sideways. When she finally stopped rolling, she felt her head for bruises and announced, "Whew, at least I didn't break my crown." Gretel decided that looked like fun so she rolled down the hill with her arms stretched out over her head, landed on Goldie's feet and laughed, "And Gretel came tumbling after."

Realizing that this was the fastest way down the hill, and also the most fun, the boys joined in as well. Holding the art case awkwardly over his head made his roll a little more difficult, but Robbie had a great time rolling down a hill for the first time in his life. They continued to climb up hills and roll down the other side until they came to the edge of a river.

None of them knew what to expect from this river, but their last river crossing was fresh in their minds and they were in no mood to attempt another one. Approximately seventy feet across, the water looked shallow in some areas with rocks jutting out of the water. In other areas, it was impossible to tell how deep the water was, but the current picked up in the middle where they could see some whitewater caps. Looking upstream, the river curved and disappeared behind the adjacent hillside. Looking downstream, the river widened, almost doubling in width before it disappeared from view beyond some trees. On the opposite river bank, the landscape looked bleak. Instead of rolling green hills, it stretched out flat and barren. Only dried up remnants of grass could be seen. Even the forest on that side of the river had an uninviting look to it, the tall trees grew close together blocking out sunlight and creating an eerie shadowy darkness.

"It looks pretty scary over there," croaked Goldilocks. "Is that the In Betweenz?"

"Yes. I think, getting there is going to be a bit of a challenge," said Blue. "I think better with food in my stomach."

Goldie passed out a piece of chicken to everyone as well as two cookies each. The canteen of fresh water was passed around. That left the apples, a few more cookies, the sandwiches and the five garlic bulbs that no one wanted to eat.

"I think we should walk downstream into the trees and look for a fallen log to use like a bridge to cross the stream," volunteered Gretel.

"I don't think so," said Hansel, "the river is wider up there and even if we found a tree long enough to reach across, we wouldn't be able to lift it. Besides, we don't know anything about this area and it could be dangerous."

"Actually, I've been here before, but only on this side. Pegasus brought me here one time," said Blue "We were searching for eucalyptus leaves for Eunice, the unicorn. She and the little ones were sick with running noses and constant sneezing. I told Pegasus eucalyptus leaves were good for colds if he knew where to find them, and this is where he brought me. He seemed to know his way around pretty well and we went over there by the trees to get the eucalyptus."

"So Pegasus and Eunice have a family together?" Robbie asked. This Land of Legends continued to amaze Robbie as he tried to understand that Blue could communicate with a horse.

"Sure, they've had several foals," explained Blue.

"And they talked to you?" Robbie asked skeptically.

"No, they don't talk to me, but they understand what I say to them," said Blue.

"Okay, eerie woods or not, I agree with Hansel that we're not going to find a tree long enough to span the river, sturdy enough for us to walk across and light enough for us to move," summarized Goldie. "So, what do we do now?"

"I could draw a bridge across. I'll make it long and sturdy and it will definitely be light," Robbie offered as a solution.

"Thanks, but no," Goldie said firmly. "How are you going to lay it across the river if you can't even see the end of the bridge? We could misjudge it and lay the end of our makeshift bridge right in the water. It's just too far across."

Hansel had been silent for a while as he studied the dry barren land on the other side of the river. Now he spoke up, "We only have half a day left before dark and we've got to cross the In Betweenz before nightfall so we can avoid the vampires and the Boogeyman. We're not due for a full moon for a few more days so I don't think we have to worry about the werewolves just now. You can see the mountaintops of the Human's Hills in the distance. The land looks flat but goes steadily uphill. Still, it should be faster and easier to walk than it was going up and down those hills, but we can't afford to waste any more time."

"Just call him," Gretel said to Blue.

"Call who?" Blue asked. Then his face lit up as he realized Gretel was referring to his winged friend. He reached into his shirt for his horn, and then blew a combination of long and short puffs resembling some sort of song. Blue could make that horn nearly as loud as a foghorn. Surely, Pegasus would hear it.

A few minutes later, Blue repeated the horn's song once again, while they waited and hoped. Hansel paced as the precious minutes ticked by.

The white speck in the distant sky grew larger and larger as Pegasus responded to Blue's call. Everyone greeted Pegasus enthusiastically as Blue rubbed Pegasus' head, and Pegasus nudged Blue affectionately with his nose. He reached into the bag and offered one of the apples to Pegasus.

Pegasus happily munched the apple as he allowed Blue to scratch between his ears. Gretel couldn't help herself as she stepped over to pet Pegasus' beautiful white coat. Robbie was intimidated by this impressive animal, but couldn't resist touching the feathers in the huge white wings.

The rest of the group remained quiet as they waited for Blue to use his gift of words to convince Pegasus to help them. Robbie saw the horse turn away from the In Betweenz in what looked like an act of defiance, but Blue was fast talking and quickly explained that they were fully prepared to cross the In Betweenz on their own, if only they could fly across the river on the back of the magnificent stallion with the majestic wings.

After more coaxing and scratching between the ears, Pegasus stretched out his front leg and ducked his head as if he were bowing. As the others watched, Blue climbed onto the horse. Pegasus jogged along the riverbank then leapt into the air. Two flaps of those mighty wings, and Pegasus was across the water and coming to a graceful landing in the shallow water on the far bank. Pegasus was quite serious about not flying over or setting foot on the dried-up ground of the In Betweenz. He stood very still until Blue slid off, then gave a nod of his beautiful head and headed back to the grassy hills on the friendly side of the river. One after another, the travelers took a turn climbing onto Pegasus' back and were flown gracefully across the water.

Robbie pretended to be polite as he allowed each of his friends to ride before him, but the truth was he had never been on a horse, not to mention a flying horse. He was quite worried he would slip off the horse's back and plunge into another terrifying river. Pegasus was returning for his last passenger, but sensed the fear in Robbie's eyes, which had turned silver with emotion. As they stared at each other, the horse's big brown eyes silently communicated understanding and trust.

Taking a deep breath, Robbie climbed on, clutched the horse's mane in a death grip, closed his eyes, and braced himself for the rough ride. He felt a jostle, then risked opening his eyes to discover the ride was over as quickly as it began. Blue helped him dismount as Pegasus dipped his head to take a long slow drink of the fresh water.

Robbie thanked Pegasus with a scratch between the ears like he had seen Blue give the horse. The rest of the gang waved goodbye to Pegasus, refilled their canteen from the river and stepped into the ungovernable lands, in a race against the sunset.

They set a quick pace and Robbie asked questions about the Human's Hills. "If Fairy Tales don't cross the In Betweenz, who lives in the Human's Hills?

Blue answered. "Fairy tales depend on the magic of Fairy Tale Town. There are other legendary people like heroes who prefer to live out in the hills where things feel a little less magical. You see, too much magic in the air makes the heroes look less impressive."

That made some sense to Robbie, but he was still puzzled, "Less impressive to who? Other heroes?"

Gretel chuckled, "They're not *all* heroes!"

Goldilocks tried to explain. "Some are ordinary townspeople from the heroes' hometowns and the villagers from legendary places like the Lost City of Camelot."

The lighthearted mood they had as they frolicked over the rolling hills was gone. The mood was more serious as the sun blazed down on this dessert wasteland. By unspoken agreement, they avoided the eerie forest that ran along the eastern border of the In Betweenz. It was just past midday so the sun was intense as they made their way north.

"I have an idea. Let's stop," said Robbie.

He pulled out his art case and retrieved his glitter crayon. He remembered making newspaper hats with his mom when they acted out Peter Pan and the pirates, so he thought he would draw a big sheet of paper and fold it into a hat. As the other children watched him flipping his hands over and under with curiosity, Robbie began to realize how difficult it was to fold origami hats with invisible paper. Frowning at the invisible crumpled mess, Robbie realized he could draw any kind of hat he wanted and drew five wide-brimmed sombreros passing them around as he drew them.

It was a refreshing moment as they laughed at each other's flattened heads that ended just above their eyes, the remainder of their heads swallowed up by the hats. The relief from the sun was immediate.

Despite the new hats, the lightened mood didn't last long as the In Betweenz sapped the happiness right out of them. The more they walked, the more irritable they became. Hansel and Gretel began to bicker as only brothers and sisters do. Gretel made the mistake of complaining about being tired.

Hansel missed no opportunity to blame his sister, "WE wouldn't be in this situation if it wasn't for YOU. You're always running headlong into mischief instead of stopping to think before you take off."

"Oh, you mean like you?" Gretel challenged. "If I waited for you to make up your mind, I'd wilt from boredom. You have to read a book, before deciding whether you like bean soup or pea soup better?"

"There's nothing wrong with taking your time and making an informed decision. Maybe if we'd spent a little more time looking for Robbie's door, we wouldn't be in this predicament," said Hansel.

"Funny, you didn't suggest that before we started out," Gretel accused.

Hansel spat back, "You didn't give me enough time to get one word out before you took off."

Goldie and Blue silently chose not to interfere with this sibling rivalry. However, Robbie's miserable expression, drooped shoulders and ears bright red with embarrassment told Hansel that he had gone too far.

Some of the color drained out of Hansel's flush face, "I'm sorry. I didn't...it's just that..."

"I'm really sorry. I didn't mean to get you involved in this mess. I looked really hard for the door. It was like looking for a needle in a haystack," Robbie apologized.

"Forget it Robbie," said Blue with his good nature returning. "You didn't force us to come. We volunteered. It could take forever to find a transparent door in that meadow. This was the only way." He put his arm on Robbie's shoulders reassuringly.

Goldie reached out and gave Robbie's arm a gentle squeeze letting him know she had no hard feelings. "It's okay," she said with a sympathetic smile. "Let's take a break."

They sat on the hot, dry ground, ate the sandwiches and passed around the canteen, each taking a small mouthful and savoring the cool water as it slipped down their throats. As Gretel tilted her head back to drink from the canteen, she felt a sharp pain on her left ankle. "Ouch!" she yelped. Then she reached over and pinched her brother.

"What did you do that for?" Hansel said, trying to keep a hold on his emotions to avoid another outburst.

"You pinched me first," yelled Gretel pointing to her ankle.

"Did not."

"Did too!"

"No, I really didn't," insisted Hansel.

"Then who did?" Gretel said and she jumped up irritably as a critter scurried away from her.

Blue bent over to try to catch it, but then straightened up quickly, "Watch out. It's a scorpion!"

"It stung me! It stung me! What do I do?" Gretel wailed.

"How do you feel?" asked Goldie.

"Okay, I guess. Let's get out of here." She started walking again and the others needed no convincing.

It wasn't long before Gretel started seeing spots of color in front of her eyes, but she kept it to herself at first. Then the dizziness started and walking became a little more difficult.

"I feel kind of funny," Gretel slurred then started to lose her balance. Robbie caught her before she hit the ground.

"I caaan't mooo maa legss," she tried to say and started to sob as she realized talking was difficult too.

"Let's get her out of the sun," Robbie said as he passed her off to Hansel and took out his glitter crayon. Although he was sick with worry, he quickly drew a tent, large enough to fit all five of them. Mindful of scorpions, he drew it complete with a floor, a tightly zippered door and reinforced edges to keep critters out. It took him all of five minutes. He hastily drew a cot and carried it inside.

Now safe from scorpions, Hansel anxiously laid Gretel on the cot. Goldie carefully poured some water from the canteen onto a handkerchief and laid it across Gretel's burning forehead. The others hovered over the cot with concern. Although none of them had any experience with watching a loved one suffer, they were familiar with human suffering from movies and the world news from the omniview. They could see Gretel's condition was bad. Hansel's theory of the Fairy Tales' being in more danger as far away as the In Betweenz now became very real to them.

Robbie felt the need to do more than watch Gretel suffer and began to fiddle with his crayon. He noticed the glitter crayon was just as shiny and beautiful as when he first discovered it. Amazingly enough, all of the drawing he had done on this trip—the whistle, the backpack, the boat, these hats, the tent and cot--hadn't worn down the crayon at all. Robbie began to draw a bench for the rest of them to sit on, but nothing happened. He reached for it and couldn't feel it. There was nothing there. It had stopped working like the other night when he tried to draw a tent. He couldn't see the specks from the sun, because there was no direct sunlight. Maybe that was it, he needed direct sunlight for his crayon to work.

He left the tent and tried again to draw the bench. Success! He carried it in to his worried friends.

Hansel had completely forgotten the bickering of the past hour as the loving concern shown visibly on his face when he looked down at his sister, no longer angry, but frightened and in pain.

Robbie couldn't be still. He broke their silence, "Do any of you know what to do for scorpion stings?"

Everybody looked toward Hansel hoping he had read a book on scorpions, or maybe there was some mention of them in the book he read about the In Betweenz. Hansel barely acknowledged the others but his very slight shake of the head let the others know that he had heard them.

Goldie volunteered, "Somehow, we've got to get the poison out."

"Where is the closest hospital?" asked Robbie.

Goldie and Blue frowned at Robbie. Blue explained, "We don't have hospitals in Fairy Tale Town. There is no need. There may be someone in the Human's Hills who can help her, but we've never been there to know for sure."

"That's still so far, and what if we can't find someone there to help her. The poison could..." Robbie didn't finish the sentence as he didn't really know what the poison would do to a Fairy Tale.

"Tell me again why you have a problem with cars?" grumbled Robbie.

"Sorry Robbie. It's the waste of petroleum, car accidents, roads all over the place, asphalt over gardens, noise pollution, all of those things" explained Blue. Silence fell again as they searched for a better answer.

Little Gretel was very still with her eyes closed. Her ankle was red and swollen. Her entire left leg was now swollen, twice the size of the right leg. It felt hot to the touch, as did her head. Her color was pale. Goldie very carefully tipped the canteen between her parted lips and tried to force her to drink, but Gretel was unable to swallow and the precious water just dribbled down her cheek.

Hansel finally stood up and scooped up his sister, "I'm taking her to Elyrise the Wise. He'll know what to do."

After all of them crawled out of the smothering hot tent, Hansel asked Blue for his whistle so he could call for Pegasus. This surprised the others who naturally assumed they would all stay together.

"I'm going with you," Blue said.

Hansel shifted the unconscious Gretel into a better position, "There is no time to waste, I've got to get going with Gretel and the rest of you need to complete Robbie's mission without us."

"You need me. We will take turns carrying Gretel, and I will whistle for Pegasus at the border. He will come to me," Blue insisted.

Hansel realized he would need Blue and gave in, but said to Robbie and Goldie, "You two must go on. We don't need you."

Goldie understood Hansel's single-minded concern and tried not to be upset by his words. She nodded her head at Hansel and put her hand on Robbie's arm. "We'll keep going," she said.

"Take care of our dear Gretel." Goldie said and kissed Gretel on her hot forehead as she handed Blue the canteen. He gave Goldie a pained look. He knew he was leaving her with no water, but Gretel was everyone's greatest concern.

"If you put her on your back, you can run faster." Robbie said as he quickly drew two strong straps to secure her to Hansel's back.

11

WHEN DARKNESS COMES

The mountains of the Human's Hills had grown larger on the horizon, but they had lost precious time taking care of Gretel and were not going to make it across the In Betweenz before darkness fell.

Robbie and Goldie hadn't talked much since the departure of Hansel, Gretel and Blue. Both of them worried about little Gretel. They were tired, but neither had wanted to stop and take another break. At least, it had started to cool off as the sun worked its way across the sky. Robbie hated being the one to decide they would have to stop for the night and set up camp in the In Betweenz, but he now knew his crayon needed sunlight and the sun was beginning to set.

Robbie took out his crayon and began to draw another tent. They had briefly discussed packing up the old tent, but Robbie could draw another one so quickly, without even whittling down his crayon so there didn't seem to be any point to that. Goldie had been determined to make it out of the In Betweenz before nightfall and had set a pace that Gretel's little legs would have had difficulty keeping up with.

Although he still had not said anything to Goldie, she saw him stop walking and start drawing and pleaded with him to push on further.

"I'm sorry," Robbie said. "We're going to need another tent to keep us safe, and my crayon needs the sunlight in order to work?" He didn't stop drawing as he explained to her.

"We can go a little further..." she started to protest, but stopped and realized how little light was left.

"What can I do to help?" she asked.

Robbie had just finished drawing the zipper and reinforcing the sides. He was starting on the first cot. "You can carry this cot in while I draw another one".

Goldie lifted the cot then had to ask Robbie where the tent was. He pointed over his shoulder, and she carried the cot in that direction until she bumped into the front of the tent. Putting the cot down, she searched the tent for the zipper, unzipped it and spread the flaps wide, then went back for the cot. Aiming for the zipper, she tried again, but got stuck again, the flaps having fallen back into place. She struggled to angle the legs in to use the cot to wedge the zipper open, but the invisible legs made this really hard to do. Tired, frustrated, worried about her friend and scared of the approaching nightfall in this ghastly land, she burst into tears and collapsed on the cot.

Hearing her sobs, Robbie froze, wondering what he was supposed to do to comfort this girl. Things had been fine when it was the five of them, he hadn't thought much about some of his new friends being girls and some boys, they were all just part of his new gang. Now that the others had left, he was alone and feeling responsible for Goldie. *This is awkward. I don't know the first thing about hanging out with a girl, least of all what to do when she cries.*

Robbie had finished drawing the second cot. He held the crayon out to Goldie who had her face buried in her hands, "Um, do you want to draw a blanket?"

Goldie only cried harder.

Do you want to draw a blanket? Robbie mocked himself. *How stupid that sounded. I should be more sensitive.*

He sat down next to her, not too close, now that this was a girl he was with and not just one of the gang. He reached up and patted her shoulder awkwardly, "There, there, please don't cry."

Robbie sat quietly criticizing himself. *There, there? Who talks like that? I feel so stupid.*

Goldie's crying stopped and she picked her head up.

Her face was streaked with tears, and Robbie thought she looked young and vulnerable despite being a fairy tale.

Goldie sensed the tension in Robbie's awkward movements, and was embarrassed that she had caused it. Making an effort to ease this tension, she reached for the crayon in his hand. "Let's see if I can draw a blanket."

She drew a large square and was feeling a little better as she concentrated on the specks in the air and reached to grab her "blanket". Her hand went right through the square and she looked at Robbie in confusion.

"You just drew the outline. You have to use the side of the crayon to shade it in." Robbie taught her.

Goldie turned the crayon and slowly and thoroughly started shading the "blanket". So involved in this task, neither had noticed that it was now full dusk when she finished the blanket. She reached for it and the top corner was very solid and hard, after that there was nothing filled in.

"I give up," she said, and handed the crayon and the blanket to Robbie.

He touched the corner that was stiff as a board and explained, "The harder you press the crayon, the more solid the object is that you created."

Feeling the other corner, he said," I guess it got too dark to finish the rest."

Reminded of how dark it now was, Goldie's fear returned and she leaped off the cot and darted into the tent, spreading the zipper for Robbie as he carried in both cots, the backpack, Elyrise's bag and his art case.

Goldie sat rigidly on the cot split between worrying about the dark night and worrying about her little friend Gretel. She had been sicker than anyone Goldie had ever seen. Thinking about fairy tales in mortal danger in this horrible land of the In Betweenz only increased Goldie's fear tenfold.

Robbie had no idea what to do as he felt rather than saw Goldie trembling in fear. Fumbling for his backpack in the darkness, he dug out the soft blanket they had all slept on the first night and wrapped it around her. He picked through the food sack. Although it had been a long time since lunch, he wasn't really hungry. He was thirsty, having had nothing to drink in the hot sun. The garlic bulbs still did not appeal to him, but the apples made his mouth water.

He took a bite of an apple and placed the other one in Goldie's hand, but she refused it.

He held it to her mouth, "Take a bite. You need the juice."

Goldie had no energy to argue. She took a bite and the juice from the succulent apple filled her mouth. She felt just a little better. "At least there is no full moon tonight, so we won't have werewolves," she said with hopefully.

Robbie tried to encourage that hope by saying, "See, not much to worry about after all."

"There are still regular wolves with long teeth, the boogeyman and vampires." The hopefulness was gone.

"They can't see us in here. We are invisible to them."

"They can still smell us. I wish we could make our scent disappear," Goldie said.

Robbie grabbed the bag excitedly, delved into it and retrieved a garlic bulb. "What about garlic?"

"Garlic!" Goldie said throwing her arms around him in a quick hug. "You're a genius!

Together, they broke up the garlic bulbs and put the pieces of cloves back in the sack, after mashing a little between their fingers so the scent would be sure to stay with them.

Robbie carried the bag to the zipper.

"Wait," Goldie said. "Don't go out there. Just toss them out."

Robbie felt he owed it to her to make her as safe as possible so he unzipped the zipper and stepped into the darkness. As he walked around the tent, he tossed the garlic out trying to create a wider border to keep the creatures away.

Being alone in the tent was ten times more frightening for Goldilocks who wondered if Robbie would be spotted and attacked by the monsters that roamed the night.

Moments later when he slipped back into the dark tent, Robbie was grabbed. Urgently, female hands reached for him and pulled him into a tight hug.

"I'm okay," he whispered and they sat down on the cot next to each other, their hands held tightly together.

Tired as they were, sleep was hard to come by. Fear was new to Goldie as she drifted back and forth between worry and terror with no intention of letting her guard down to go to sleep. It was the scariest night Robbie had ever had, worrying about vampires, and boogeymen, which apparently did exist in this crazy Land of Legends. He listened to the sound of the evening not knowing what other creatures of the night were out there. He could hear the owls and the wolves whose howls seemed to get closer and closer as he listened. He only hoped the garlic would throw off their scent, and the invisible tent would keep them safely hidden. He tried to convince himself they were safe. As long as the creatures that walked the night didn't accidentally bump into the tent...

It sounded like the wolves were only a few feet away, Goldie squeezed his hand harder and buried her face in his neck. Robbie let go of one of her hands to put his arm around her and hold her closer, trying to draw security from the nearness of another person.

He put his hand on her cheek as he leaned into her to whisper right in her ear. "I'm sorry," he said faintly, afraid to say anymore even as he realized the wetness on his finger meant that she had tears on her cheeks.

She only squeezed his hand harder.

The night dragged on as the nightmarish thoughts continued to haunt them. Although they were afraid to sleep during the long night, it was hard to tell whether the sound of the howling wolves running amongst noisy barks and growls was real or, in fact, a nightmare. Their hearts nearly stopped when they heard the sound of an animal screeching as it was likely captured and eaten by an even bigger creature.

12

THE HUMAN'S HILLS

It was still early in the morning when Robbie and Goldie reached the end of the In Betweenz. Unable to sleep during the long, terrifying night, they had started their journey shortly after sunrise. With the sunlight, Robbie's awareness of being alone with a girl had returned and some of the awkwardness returned with it. They had eaten the last two apples in silence and said very little during the morning walk. Now, they stood staring at the beautiful Human's Hills which rose up majestically in front of them, right on the other side of a very deep gorge.

If they hadn't been in such a hurry to leave the horrific In Betweenz, Robbie would have wanted to stop and sketch the gorgeous landscape in front of him. Now, their one thought was how to cross the gorge. After walking along the gorge for about thirty minutes trying to find the best place to cross, they settled on a spot where the gorge was only six feet wide.

"If we took a running start, we could make it, no problem," suggested Robbie.

"I'm not so sure," said Goldie who didn't like the idea of jumping too short and falling into the gorge. It was a long way down—more than 10 stories.

Robbie moved back from the deadly drop and placed two rocks on the ground about six feet apart. "Okay, let's practice."

He got a running start, planted his foot at the first rock and cleared the second with a couple feet to spare. "Hmmm, maybe eight feet. That should do it. Now, you try."

Goldie ran as fast as she could and jumped into the air just clearing the second rock. Thinking it too close for comfort, she tried again, but this time, landed and fell backward into the pretend gorge. She tried again, and again fell backward, her dress in a most unladylike heap.

"One out of three times, Robbie. I don't like these odds. There's got to be another way."

Robbie took out his magic crayon and started drawing.

She sat down to watch him draw.

Robbie had trouble looking at her as he said, "About last night..."

She cut him off, "It's over Robbie, we made it."

He did look up now, "Goldie, I'm sorry. I feel like all I do is put my friends in danger."

"We survived," she pointed out.

"I made you cry. I feel terrible. I really am sorry."

"I admit I was scared, terrified actually." She shuddered, then shook it off, "But you were brave, and I was so glad to have you with me. I couldn't have made it without you."

Robbie felt his throat tighten and his eyes get watery as he looked down at the hand she had wrapped around his arm. He looked away. He hadn't cried in seven years, ever since his sixth birthday party that got cancelled. He wasn't about to start crying now, in front of a girl. He just couldn't understand how these friends could care so much, how they put themselves in danger just to help him out.

Not knowing what to say, he said nothing and bowed his head.

Goldie squeezed his arm and removed her hand. Robbie got back to work and finished the bridge he was drawing.

When finished, the bridge was about nine feet long. Robbie slid it across the gorge.

"Is it a bridge?" Goldie asked

"Yep."

"Is it sturdy?"

"I made the lines really dark to reinforce it. It's about two feet wide so you should have good balance."

"Robbie, I don't know about this. You expect us to walk across an invisible board. One misstep and we take a long fall."

"Don't worry. I drew sides on this bridge each a few inches high. Just shuffle your feet along so you can feel the sides and you'll be fine."

Robbie went first to prove the bridge was sturdy.

"Now it's your turn," he waited expectantly for Goldie.

Goldie held her breath and inched her way across. Robbie watched her walk on thin air over the one hundred foot drop. As used to the invisible crayon as he'd become, some things still looked odd.

Safe on the other side of the bridge, she fell into his arms. After a brief moment, Robbie straightened up and pushed her away, a bit embarrassed by this display now that the night terrors were over.

Goldie sensed his discomfort and knew the closeness of the last night had been more about terror than true feelings.

"Should we leave something to mark the bridge so we can use it for the way back?" Goldie suggested, masking her disappointment.

Robbie paled at the thought that they would soon be returning to the In Betweenz. That is, if all went well with his mission. He wished he could wait years before returning to the In Betweenz, but on the other hand, he hoped they could find the painting quickly and return to the In Betweenz at dawn tomorrow. They would get an early start so they would not run out of sunlight.

Robbie shivered as he thought of all the creepy things that haunted the night. He shoved the bridge into the gorge, preventing the horrid things from following them.

This side of the gorge was as full of live growing plants as the In Betweenz was barren. Bordering the gorge were thick weeds—sweet smelling honeysuckle, raspberry bushes bursting with the ripe red fruit and what Goldie thought was poison sumac surrounding the raspberries. They spent a few minutes stuffing the sweet red seedy fruit into their mouths, careful to avoid the purplish poison berries. Robbie had tasted raspberries from the market before, but he had never experienced the pleasure of picking his own fruit off the vine and letting the fresh flavor of the berries pop in his mouth. After ten minutes, he was all scratched up by the thorns on the raspberry bushes and had accidentally touched the sumac bushes more times than he could count. He sincerely hoped Goldie was wrong about sumac berries causing a poisonous, itchy rash. He didn't feel itchy, but had avoided eating the purplish berries out of respect for Goldie's concern, even though they reminded him so much of tiny blueberries which he loved.

The shrubs were thick and they spent some time crawling under and over thorn bushes and tangled vines. Apparently, few people from the Human's Hills went into or came out of the In Betweenz. Thinking of all the terror they had just experienced, Robbie could certainly understand why.

A short distance into the underbrush and the In Betweenz were completely obscured from view. They didn't know where they were going, but they could see trees a few yards ahead and hoped they might be able to move better in the forest than in these sticker bushes. Eventually, the thick weeds thinned and they found themselves in a light and airy forest where walking became much easier. Unlike the dark and eerie forest of the In Betweenz, this forest was beautiful. Sunlight was shining through the branches, and a light breeze was blowing the leaves. The friends felt lighthearted again and began skipping through the woods, laughing at themselves and each other. As they came to the edge of the forest, they could see the town and the mountains beyond it.

This land was beautiful. Robbie couldn't resist taking out his sketch-pad. Goldie took the opportunity to lean against a tree and close her eyes for a much needed catnap. Robbie tried to sketch everything he'd seen this side of the gorge, from the raspberry fields to this beautiful town sitting at the base of the mountains. The town was quaint, the buildings nestled together, much closer than what he had seen in Fairy Tale Town. It was a fairly large town, but much too small to be called a city by modern standards. It was nothing like his own Rosecrest City, because there were no skyscrapers, no apartment buildings, no pollution and no traffic noises.

Even more impressive than this picturesque town, were the huge mountains that provided a backdrop towering above it. Seeing real mountains dotted with cascading waterfalls took his breath away. He allowed himself twenty minutes to sketch, convincing himself that Goldie needed the rest.

"Amazing," remarked Robbie having finished his sketches, "I've never seen mountains before, except in pictures."

"Beautiful," agreed Goldie staring at the impressive mountains which she'd heard about all her life and was finally looking at.

"So now that we've reached the Human's Hills, what next?" asked Goldie.

Robbie had no idea. He flipped back a few pages in the sketchbook to the rhyme. Reading aloud, he hoped it would make more sense now.

"Over the hills through the In Betweenz
You will find out what this task means
Find answers long sought out
And bring back a treasure beyond a doubt."

"Does that help you?" asked Goldie.

Robbie shook his head, "I think we should head into town and see if anyone knows how we can get a painting by *pierres*."

The first street they crossed on their way into town was lined with Victorian style houses. He loved the cheerfully painted houses with the brightly colored trim, the odd angles and the tower rooms complete with cupolas above them. Some had widow walks on their roofs. All of the houses on the street had white picket fences, beautiful landscaping, wide front porches with porch swings and flower boxes on the railings.

Robbie stopped the first person that walked past them. "Excuse me. Where might I find an Art Emporium?" he asked. The man looked at him as if he were crazy and walked away.

Robbie muttered, "The man is wearing leggings and a..." He wasn't sure what to call the shirt dress which extended to his mid-thigh, "...a tunic, and he thinks I'm crazy!" For the first time since he started, he was directionless. Always before, he had known the purpose of his journey—first to return home, then to get a Transparency detector, then to get to the Forest of Money and finally to get through the In Betweenz and then to the Human's Hills. Well, here he was in the Human's Hills, and he had no idea what to do next. How was he supposed to find this painting?

Goldie linked her arm through Robbie's, refusing to let her high spirits dampen as she anticipated exploring this adorable little town.

The central part of town reminded Robbie of his own Bell Street with an old-fashioned bakery, bookstore, specialty shops, a mom-and-pop convenience store, a candy store and an apothecary. Naturally, the street was called Main Street. To be specific, there were two one-way streets, East Main Street and West Main Street which were divided by a grassy park running down the center. It was not a very busy street, since Robbie hadn't seen any cars in this town either. People were either walking or riding bikes. Some of the bikes were pulling sleds on large wheels using some pulley and fan system, but only moving as fast as ten miles an hour. The bikers were wearing modern looking tight-fitting outfits and were lean and muscular. Now that he noticed, all of the people he saw seemed to be in excellent physical shape. *Maybe it had to do with all the exercise they were getting*, he thought to himself.

It was a large park and full of families. Some were pushing beautiful old-fashioned baby carriages. Others had large woven baskets and were having picnics on blankets in the grass. Some were merely strolling along. A huge fountain sat in the middle of the park surrounded by benches. There was an old lady sitting on one of the benches throwing birdseeds to a group of pigeons. An old man sat next to her comfortably reading a newspaper. On another bench sat an elegantly dressed couple, the lady shielding the sun with a parasol whose dangling ribbons matched her long skirt. There were several stone tables with pairs of people concentrating over chess sets. The scene reminded him more than a little of a story he'd read but couldn't quite recall.

Goldie rushed over to assist a toddler who was frustrated because the truck he was pulling with a string had been overturned and his mother was involved in a conversation with another young woman and hadn't noticed.

Robbie took out his sketchbook to draw this cozy park. As he watched the families, he imagined what it would have been like to go on a picnic in the park with his own mom and dad. He could picture himself sitting there on the blanket, his mother handing him food from a picnic basket. The spell was broken when he tried to picture his father next to him, since he had never seen so much as a picture of his father.

Goldie kicked off her shoes and said, "Come on."

He did not get up, but watched her frolicking in the shallow fountain with some children. The sun shone down on her hair lighting up the gold like a halo, joy evident in her whole body as she entertained the children. Robbie realized how truly beautiful Goldilocks was as he watched her play so unselfconsciously.

Something above Goldie's head caught Robbie's eye, bringing him out of his reverie. There was a paintbrush on the sign of the building behind the fountain.

He was on his feet instantly, pointing out the sign to Goldie.

Goldie stepped out of the fountain. "You go," she said as she looked down at the soaking wet hem of her dress. "I'm a bit too soggy for an art gallery right now."

Racing across the street, Robbie narrowly avoided getting run over by a bicycle with a bell.

The art museum was small and full of beautiful marble statues. Robbie loved the statues, but quickly looked for paintings. The gallery assistant hurried over. After the tunic and the other old-fashioned looking clothes in the park, Robbie was surprised to see that he was wearing denim jeans and a black leather jacket, with black leather boots.

"I'm looking to buy a painting," Robbie said. "I am looking for something by a particular artist."

"We don't sell paintings here," the assistant interrupted Robbie.

"But you have a paintbrush on your sign," Robbie challenged.

"You can try the market place," the assistant said dismissively, nodding toward the door.

"Please, I've come a long way and I don't know how to find the marketplace," Robbie tried again."

The docent turned his nose up at Robbie, "We don't sell paintings. Try the marketplace in Town Square!" he said the last part emphatically as he opened the door, practically shoving Robbie out the door.

Robbie found Goldie playing a hopscotch game with some younger girls. The bottom of her dress was still very wet from the fountain, but Goldie did not seem to mind. "Any luck?" she asked.

Robbie shook his head and told her about the marketplace in Town Square.

"So how do we get to Town Square?"

One of the little girls from the hopscotch game said, "I know where it is. My daddy sells sausages there."

Robbie and Goldie turned onto Municipal Street just as the little girl had directed.

The architecture was very different on this street, representing a third time period. It was as if the Human's Hills was a patchwork quilt with each patch representing a glimpse of a different time period. Instead of the Victorian houses on the edge of town, or the quaint shops on Main Street straight out of a 1920's painting, this street presented immense, stately buildings including a courthouse, a jailhouse, a huge bank, a library three stories high and a museum. These grey stone buildings featured sculpted elaborate trim and were topped with statues and gargoyles, with rooflines like castles all crowded together on the same street, each building fighting to stand out from the next.

Robbie looked longingly at the Museum of History longing to satisfy his growing curiosity about this strange town.

Goldie read his mind and said, "You would never be satisfied with just a glance, and we've got to find this painting and return to the Forest of Money so we can get your Transparency detector and get you back home to your mother. Besides, the sooner we get back, the sooner we can find out about Gretel. I can't stop thinking about her?"

Robbie was worried about Gretel too and hoped she had recovered from her scorpion sting. He was still trying to wrap his head around the immortality of *inpilquing*, just as his friends were questioning if straying beyond the borders of Fairy Tale Town threatened this immortality, and how? Could she lose a leg or suffer from everlasting pain and agony? She was such a brave little girl, and he really hoped his journey hadn't caused her lasting misery, or worse.

Municipal Street was clearly the business district of this area, with this street looking more like a city than a town. The blocks were shorter like city blocks, but there were so many of them. Goldie and Robbie had stopped to drink from the refreshing water fountains in the park, but their stomachs were now growling and they knew they would need to spend some of their money on food. For the moment they ignored their protesting bellies, having no idea how much their painting would cost.

Still following the girl's directions, they turned onto Jones Street and headed toward the mountains. It felt as if they entered yet another time period. The houses on this street were very modern with glass fronts, steel beams, sharp angles and multiple rooflines.

"What's with the collage of time periods in the Human's Hills?" Robbie asked, an eyebrow arched like the angled building behind him.

Goldie had no reply. She merely shrugged her shoulders and tucked a lock of the golden hair behind her ear. They had been walking in relative silence, but it was not awkward. The two friends were at ease with each other and felt no need to fill the silence. Goldie and the others were now his best friends. Real friends, not characters in the plays he and his mother made up, not kids in school who were nice to your face, but never invited you out to play with them or called you on the phone. It occurred to him that when he found the painting, he'd be one step closer to going home to his mother, and one step closer to leaving his new friends behind.

Robbie heard a well-dressed woman yelling at a frazzled foreman at a construction site of a modern house being built entirely of glass. He was pulling on his already messed up hair, reminding her that they wouldn't be so far behind schedule if she didn't keep breaking the glass panels. While Robbie and Goldie watched, the angry woman swung her purse at the burly foreman who blocked the attack with his clipboard. She then leaned over and grabbed a stone, hurling it at the foreman. She narrowly missed hitting him in the eye, but squarely hit the center of a huge glass pane as her escort hauled her off in a bicycle powered buggy. The glass cracked in eight different directions sending a single crack line in each direction. As all eyes watched in horror, the crack lines simultaneously spider webbed out from the core then erupted into a shower of glass pouring out over the workmen who had been preparing to set the glass in place.

As the buggy was pedaled away, the foreman groaned loudly. "Good thing we ordered a spare panel this time," he said to his crew. The scared crew unfroze and appreciated the foreman's foresight. One spoke up, "Does anyone remember where we hid it from her?" They looked toward the hard dirt in the back yard of the construction site and began to scratch and shake their heads.

The foreman yelled, "Get the Transparency detector".

Robbie and Goldie stared as one of the workmen brought out a large handheld silver device shaped a bit like a wheelbarrow. Instead of a basket, it had a circular disk that resembled a fan. This could be the solution to all of his problems. If he could just borrow this contraption and take it back to his green meadow, he could find his door and get back to his world—the world of his mother. He wondered if it would be wrong to spend Elyrise's fifty dollars if he didn't complete his mission, but it was unlikely he could borrow it for fifty dollars. Besides, borrowing this implied a return trip to the Human's Hills which was not in the plan.

The kids crossed to the backyard where they were able to get a better look at the man holding the Transparency detector. He had crossed into a taped off section of the yard and was slowly swinging the Transparency detector in large sweeping motions as it hovered above the ground. The dirt blew around and the small pebbles and bits of debris laying in the dirt were projected above it in holographic form as the air whisked from the bottom of the fan. The whishing sound was replaced by a more resonant sound as the holographic image took the shape of the flat smooth surface of the corner of a large panel of glass.

"I found it" yelled the worker as he turned around to yell for assistance, only then noticing his visitors.

Hey, what were you doing standing there? There's no trespassing on this construction site."

Robbie met his directness with directness of his own, "We wanted to see how it worked," blurted out Robbie with a nod to the Transparency detector.

The workman was proud to have the honor of operating the fancy machinery and softened at the kids. "Pretty impressive, huh?"

"How does it work?" Goldie wanted to know.

"Inside the fan is a large diamond that projects the deflected particles through the diamond prism resulting in the holograms you saw," explained the workman.

"We need one," Robbie stated.

"Sorry kid," said the workman. "This is not going anywhere until this job is finished, especially since these are so valuable and rare."

13

THE MARKETPLACE

The marketplace was huge, and fantastic! There was a massive collection of booths spread out in front of him as far as the eye could see. Anything and everything was available for purchase, and there was no particular order to it. As they walked from vendor to vendor, they saw jewelry, sweaters, pots, fancy vases, sausages, dog leashes, toe socks, porcelain trinkets, live animals and a book vendor. Robbie took a few seconds to scan this one out of curiosity. He saw some of the classics from his time, *Romeo and Juliet, Great Expectations, Tom Sawyer*. Robbie also saw some interesting new titles, *Horrors of the In Betweenz, Legends of the Legends, The History of the Human's Hills* and countless others. He held up a copy of *Goldilocks and the Three Bears*, and Goldie blushed and moved to the next booth displaying its colorful scarves.

"Look, this place is huge. Finding a painting by *pierres* will be like finding two snowflakes that match. I have no idea where to start," said Robbie.

"Excuse me," Goldie said to the vendor of blown glass baubles. "When does the marketplace close?"

The vendor squinted into the sun, "Looks like you have about an hour before we close. The booths are closed up and taken down in the late afternoon so that we are home well before sundown. Not to worry, the market will reopen again next week as always."

"Next week?" Robbie squeaked out in a panicked voice.

The vendor did not notice Robbie's comment or his reaction, he was intent on making a sale. "I think these blue baubles are the perfect color earrings for you" he said as he held some earrings up to Goldie's ears.

Goldie took a step back away from the earrings. "They're lovely, but I wasn't looking for earrings. We are looking for a painting by *pierres*. Do you know where we might find one?"

The vendor looked quizzical for a moment, "No, can't recall that name. There are almost a dozen art vendors selling paintings today. Have a look around."

"We better split up if we're going to cover this territory and find this painting. You take this side and I'll take that side," Robbie said pointing to where he would start. We'll meet in the middle when we're finished and find something to eat."

Robbie ripped a page out of his sketchbook and began to sketch. In moments, he had a second rough sketch of *pierres*' drawing. He handed the sketchbook over to Goldie, "Show this to the art vendors and ask if they've seen the original painting by *pierres*. Hopefully, they will be able to show us something else by the same artist."

Robbie had shown his sketch around and been sent to four different art booths, each one seemed as far as possible from the last booth as he zigzagged around the market place. He started to get worried that he wouldn't get through the marketplace before it closed up for the night, actually, for the week!

In his haste, Robbie brushed past a severe looking woman with a high collar so stiff it could hold up her head without the help of her neck. She carried a striking painting under her arm with features recognizable enough to stop Robbie in his tracks.

"May I help you," she asked pretentiously, staring down her long nose at Robbie.

"Where did you get that painting?" asked Robbie who had met a lot of pretentious women in the theater world and did not scare off that easily.

"Over there," she said and pointed toward a booth two rows away that was already cleaning up for the evening.

Robbie took off running intent on reaching the booth before closing. So intent was he on his goal that he knocked over a man and sent him sprawling. He muttered a brief apology with no time to stop and offer assistance. He did not hear the man call out after him.

The portable walls were bare as the vendor continued packing up his wagon. Only a single painting propped up against the booth, some miniature portraits and some pencil sketches, remained to be put away. Robbie set down his art case and bent down to get a closer look at the landscape painting on the ground. He recognized the same mountains and the artist's particular use of colors, only this painting had a dragon flying over the mountain, poised to dive into the cascading waterfall. Sure enough, it was signed *pierres*. Carefully turning it over, he read a shocking price tag: $1,875.

Goldie spied Robbie and called out to him. He looked up, anxious to show her what he'd found. She was walking toward him with two huge sausages on sticks that instantly made his mouth water and his stomach growl, reminding him just how long it had been since he'd eaten.

At the same time, the man Robbie had knocked over in his haste had caught up to him, dragging a policeman with him.

"There he is—the thief!" The man complained loudly to the policeman that the boy was running away like a thief when he knocked him over and didn't even stop to help him.

"Is this true?" asked the policeman. Still holding the valuable painting, Robbie was confused and couldn't find his voice.

A crowd of men from the market had gathered around including the art vendor who paused in packing up his booth even as some dark clouds moved in. Robbie looked around for Goldie but could no longer see her through the throng of the crowd. He was grabbed roughly, the painting taken away as his hands were held behind his back. "I am going to need to search you," informed the policeman.

"That's my sketch! Thief!" yelled the art vendor who saw the paper in Robbie's hand with the torn holes in the top of it just like those on display at his booth. Similar sketches that *pierres* had similarly torn out of a sketchbook.

The policeman looked at the sketch in Robbie's hand which was indeed similar to the sketches lying on the booth and picked up the small sign indicating they were $150 apiece. In fact, there were several sketches of the same scene Robbie had drawn. Only someone with Robbie's artistic skill would notice the subtle differences between his sketch and those done by *pierres*. Unfortunately, the art vendor lacked that skill.

The angry man continued to rant and rave about the thief who had knocked him over, crushing his new hat. The crowd was closing in on Robbie, people yelling to each other asking who the thief was and had anyone ever seen him before. Goldie tried to push through the thick crowd forgetting about the sausages she was still holding, but people would not make way for her. She called out Robbie's name just as thunder rumbled directly overhead. The policeman shouted questions at Robbie that he could no longer hear as his head began to swim, his empty stomach growled and his mouth felt unconnected to his body.

His day became a collage in front of him from barren hills of the In Betweenz, deep gorges, a park full of people, streets of stately architecture, modern glass houses, the booths of the market, pictures of landscapes, colors, violet, cerulean, ochre, rust...

Robbie fainted.

As the policeman started to drag away Robbie's unconscious form, the clouds burst and the rain poured down. Goldie called out to the policeman, pleading for him to release Robbie, but nobody heard her over the ruckus. He dragged Robbie away so quickly, Goldie couldn't even get around the crowd before the two were swallowed up in the crowds of the marketplace. With the departure of the policeman, the excitement ended and the noisy, throbbing press of the crowd quickly dispersed. Robbie was nowhere to be seen.

Goldie looked in each direction trying to decide which way to go after Robbie, when out of the corner of her eye, she spotted something familiar. It was Robbie's beloved art case. Of course, he wasn't able to grab it when he was dragged off unconscious. He had left it right in front of the booth from which he had been dragged away. Just as Goldie ran under the booth's awning and bent down to retrieve it, she noticed the dragon in the beautiful piece of art sitting on the ground propped up against the booth. She was no artist, but it was a landscape that reminded her of the one in the sketchbook she had been carrying around. She examined the mountains and the waterfall and the cabin cozily nestled into the hillside. The dragon was definitely new. The art vendor who had been interrupted in his efforts to clean up his booth before the cloudburst, was scurrying to the front of the booth to gather up the last three paintings. The overhang of the table and the overhead tent had protected them from the sudden downpour.

Almost finished with his packing, the vendor finally noticed Goldie staring at the landscape painting and thought he might make one final sale before closing, "Isn't it beautiful? This is one of my favorites."

Goldie would not even look at this man who got Robbie arrested, and she was definitely too afraid to pull out the sketchbook to compare it with the painting. She wished she had studied the painting as Robbie had. It was then she saw the signature obscured in the corner, *pierres*. She gasped.

The vendor's eye shone merrily, "This is from one of our local artists, a favorite of the King's. He uses the Human's Hills as his inspiration for many of his paintings," he said as he admired the painting himself.

"This artist, would he happen to be here today?" Goldie asked tightly, preferring to do business with the artist rather than this mean man.

The vendor laughed, "No. He lives a private life. He rarely comes down into town. Lucky for you, I have several of his paintings available for purchase."

Goldie felt the money she was carrying. Just forty-five dollars left after buying the sausages. Was it right for her to purchase a painting so she and Robbie could return to Elyrise and end this mission? After all, it was Robbie's test.

The vendor was anxiously awaiting her answer so he could finish closing up his booth. The rain was still pounding on the roof of the tent and if the wind picked up, the pictures could be ruined.

Goldie said, "I must find my friend. It is for him to decide."

"Well, where is he then? I need to finish closing up."

"I'm hoping you will tell me. See, he was the boy dragged away by the policeman. Where would he be taken? Do you know what might happen to him?" asked Goldie nervously.

"The thief?" His voice became angry. Goldie slid around to put her body between the nasty vendor and Robbie's art case so the unreasonable man would not try to claim that as well. "You mean he wants to steal one of my pictures, not buy one? Well lucky for me, he will be locked in the city jail and won't get out before the morning light." Irritated, he moved away from Goldie and leaned down to resume packing up his paintings.

Goldie noticed the one remaining table under the tent still had a few sketches on it, though the rest of the items on the table, including any sign of the price, had been cleaned up for the night. To her untrained eye, they sure looked like the sketches Robbie drew. In fact, several of them still had the holes in the top where they had been torn from a sketchbook. The smudges of dirt on one of them convinced her that it was in fact Robbie's picture the policeman had returned to the vendor.

"How much are you asking for this drawing?" she said, thinking she might like to have Robbie's picture back.

"Those sketches are one fifty," he said.

Goldie had little experience buying art, but thought that was a fair price for something that took Robbie two minutes to sketch. She reached for the moneybag from Elyrise, "And how much is the one in your hands?"

"Eighteen seventy-five."

She offered the vendor a twenty-dollar bill, hoping Robbie would be pleased that she had completed his mission for him.

"What is this?" he bellowed. "You insult me with this! This painting is worth one thousand, eight hundred, seventy-five dollars!' For eighteen dollars and seventy-five cents, I won't even tell you where the artist lives!"

Goldie was shocked by the staggering price tag. She did not understand why Elyrise, who grew money, had given them so little cash to purchase a painting he obviously knew would cost so much. She grasped the only morsel of hope she had heard and held out two twenty-dollar bills, letting the man see that she had a mere five dollars left in her money pouch, "You know where the artist lives?"

The greedy vendor grabbed at the easy money, spared her only one more second of his time as he pointed to the tiny cabin in the landscape painting. "Right there," he said smugly, trying to offer as little help as possible while justifying to himself that he had earned the forty dollars.

He then grabbed the remaining items of art and packed them in his wagon.

Angry that she had been tricked out of most of their money, Goldie reached down and grabbed Robbie's art case, shifted the invisible bookbag on her back, slid the sketchbook inside the case for safe-keeping and stepped out into the rain.

14

GOLDILOCKS FINDS HELP

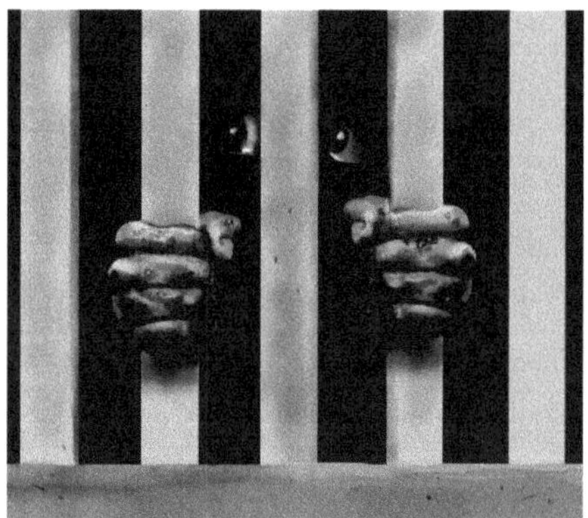

Robbie noticed two things upon awakening. One, he was hot, hungry, itchy and in general, very uncomfortable. Two, it was pitch dark. He gave himself a decent scratching then lay very still for a moment as he tried to remember where he was and what had happened. *A jail cell!* Suddenly, it all came back to him. The market place, the man yelling "thief." The policeman searching him, and then everything going fuzzy. He remembered regaining consciousness as he was dragged off, then tossed in this cell.

Robbie didn't know the laws in the LOL, but the policeman who dragged him away, refused to talk to him and just threw him in a dark jail cell. Robbie had been hungry and exhausted and quickly fell asleep on the hard bench.

He felt around for his art case, *maybe he could draw his way out of this*. He couldn't find the box or his backpack. Panic set in even at the same time he realized his art case wouldn't help him, because the crayon didn't work in the dark. Robbie went to the bars and yelled, "Hey", but his nervous voice produced nothing but a squeak. He cleared his throat and tried again, gradually getting louder and louder, trying to be heard.

"Aww, come on kid. Knock it off and go back to sleep," complained a groggy voice.

"Who's that?" asked Robbie nervously.

"The boogeyman. Who do you think kid? Go back to sleep. Nobody's coming in here again until the morning."

Robbie lay back down, but for the second time this journey, sleep eluded him. Only this time, he didn't have Goldie by his side. He felt more alone than he had ever felt in his life.

In the morning, Robbie was taken to a small room with a window, a chair, and more bars. After the darkness of his cell, the morning light coming in through the small window was nearly blinding.

"Robbie!" Goldie exclaimed.

Robbie turned toward the sound as his vision returned. "Goldie! Boy, are you a sight for sore eyes," he beamed at her, still scratching his itchy face, arms and hands.

She hurried to him with her arms extended, then stopped a foot in front of him, taking in his exhaustion and his red bumpy rash on every inch of the exposed skin on his hands, arms and face.

"Oh no, you look terrible! Don't scratch. You have poison sumac, and scratching only makes the rash spread!"

Robbie had a thousand questions for her, "How did you find me? Where did you spend the night? How do I get out of here?"

"Well, I'm still working on the last one. How about I start at the beginning, and you stop scratching?" As she said this, she reached out gently grasping both of his hands, preventing him from doing further damage, and began her story...

Fortunately, after the policeman dragged you away, the rain stopped as quickly as it had started. That nasty art vendor would not sell me one of his overpriced paintings, or even a sketch, but he did tell me that the artist lived in the cabin in the picture! I just had to find you first. I found the jail on Municipal Street easily enough, but it was locked up tight for the night and no one would respond to me no matter how hard I pounded. I didn't know what to do and sincerely wished LBB was still with me since he's the one that's good at thinking on his feet.

I sat down on the curb and pulled my knees up to my chin to come up with a plan. I thought of basic necessities, *Food, water, shelter*. The sausage I bought at the marketplace sat heavy in my stomach, and I wanted nothing else to eat or drink. As for shelter, I thought I could head back to the marketplace and crawl up in a vacant booth for the night if I had to. Despite the mix up at the marketplace that landed you in jail, I refused to give up hope that we could clear up everything in the morning.

The sun was getting lower on the horizon, and I estimated a little more than an hour until it was fully dark. The museum across the street looked beautiful with the sun setting beyond it. Even the architecture of the jail was pleasing to look at in the glow of the late sun. I hoped for your sake, it was nice on the inside of the jail as well. I thought about climbing the stairs of the museum to sleep on the terrace under the stars. Maybe I would sleep in the cupola on the roof of the museum. It was so warm, I thought about climbing that purple mountain and just falling asleep under the stars watching the beautiful waterfall trickle down the hillside? I giggled to myself as I saw the outline of the mountains already resembled a sleeping giant.

Then I experienced a sense of *déjà vu*. I knew I had looked at that scene before. Robbie, it was the scene in *pierres*' landscape!

I darted across the street, past the museum, to get a better view. I stood at the base as the towering mountain rose up in front of me. About halfway up, nestled amongst the trees, was a cabin. It was the cabin from the painting!

I never made a conscious decision to start climbing, but I started up that mountain as quickly as I could, knowing I had to reach that cabin before full dark. I passed a few children coming down the mountain and tried to ask them if they knew *pierres*, but they were chatting loudly to each other and did not even pause to answer me. The trail wasn't all that difficult, but it was getting dark. Finally, I met a boy coming down. He had jet-black hair and reminded me a little of you.

I asked him who lived in the cabin, he said, "That is Monsieur's cabin, but he is no longer at home. Monsieur finished my portrait and took off."

The boy explained. "Sometimes when he finishes a portrait, he is moody and disappears for days."

He suggested I come back another day, but with darkness setting in, I had no choice but to keep on going.

When I got to the cabin, I knocked on the door and called out, but nobody answered. The door was unlocked so I went in. (She winked at Robbie reminding him that the story of Goldilocks started with a girl entering an unlocked cabin.) The cabin was small and sparsely furnished so I could see immediately that nobody was home. It had a small kitchen with a table that also doubled as a countertop and cutting board. He had his own Omniview. Nobody in Fairy Tale Town has their own Omniview! They are rare and expensive.

Beyond the Omniview were a bed, a lounge chair, and a straight-backed chair that sat in front of two easels. On the back wall were many windows and the stars were beginning to sparkle in the early evening light. It was a beautiful view.

There was another chair set up on the other side of the easels. On the first easel, sat an unfinished landscape in *pierres*' now familiar style. It featured a close-up view of a waterfall so detailed and intricate that the splashing water seemed to move—as though alive. On the second easel, sat a finished portrait of the boy I spoke to on the trail. The brush was still wet so I know I had just missed the artist.

I hoped he would return soon, so I occupied myself looking at the dozens of portraits packed side by side on each of the walls. There were also scenes from fairy tales--Cinderella, Beauty and the Beast, Peter

Pan. The paintings were amazing. It was as if you could see exactly how they were feeling. And the scenes were so detailed.

I thought about watching the Omniview. It was the first time in my life that I could have control of the 15,000 channels of the Omniview. I know people in the Land of Legends are encouraged to watch other civilizations and learn from their mistakes, but I've always felt like it was spying on unknowing people. I chose to pass the time studying the portraits.

Many of the paintings were of the same person—a young lady about twenty years old, with sleek raven black hair. She had piercing green eyes and a captivating smile—she was breathtaking. This same lady was included in each of the fairy tale scenes with the same piercing green eyes despite different costumes, hair and makeup. The artist seemed to be obsessed with her. There were even portraits of her by herself doing ordinary things like sitting at a kitchen chair, brushing her hair, walking in a park.

After the raven-haired beauty, there was a portrait of a little baby wrapped in a blanket. This was followed by portraits of children, some girls, some boys. The portraits progressed in age from infancy to a young teenager. A few of the portraits looked like they could be of the same person, but most of the portraits varied in hair color, eye color, and stature. I saw those piercing green eyes in a few of the children and wondered if they were related to the raven-haired beauty *pierres* favored.

He still hadn't come home, so I tucked your art case against the lounge chair, and set the invisible backpack on top of it. Exhausted, I laid down on the bed, but it was too soft, the straight back chair was too hard so I curled up in the lounge chair that was *just right*.

The next thing I knew, it was morning. I was startled awake when the door to the cabin opened and light flooded the room. It took me a minute to remember where I was. A man in his twenties, entered. At first, he didn't notice me curled up in the chair as he walked to the kitchen counter to deposit the fresh fish he was carrying.

Finding the artist who could finally end our journey made me so nervous, I couldn't find my voice. He was tall and lean with sad eyes. He had long straw-colored hair, tied back with a string. Something about his eyes struck me, but I couldn't see beyond the sadness in them.

Then he saw me. Momentarily startled, he dropped the knife that he had just picked up, onto the floor, barely missing his shoe. He recovered quickly. His face transformed, and the sadness in his eyes seemed to be whisked behind a quickly pulled curtain. He smiled at me as he picked up his knife and began scaling the fish.

I must say I was happily surprised by his reaction since we haven't experienced a lot of kindness from the adults in these Human's Hills. Clearly, he did not seem to mind my uninvited visit.

I asked, "Are you *pierres*?"

He chuckled and explained, "I am Pierre S." He paused emphatically before and after the S. "Might you be Goldilocks?"

I nodded, used to being recognized, at least until I came to these Human's Hills.

"I need your help. My friend is in jail and we need one of your paintings, and we have no money, and you weren't home..." My words tumbled out of me like the water in the painting on Pierre's easel.

He was so nice. He invited me to breakfast, apologizing for not having porridge to offer me. Pierre told me that despite his location, he gets lots of visitors, particularly from the children of the town who take art lessons.

As he made breakfast, I told him the story of what had happened in the marketplace when we were looking for his pictures and how I ended up coming to find him.

He gestured toward the easel with the portrait of the boy on it, "I often go on fishing trips to clear my head after finishing one of the portraits for my personal collection. Lucky for you, the fish were biting this morning and I decided to return home." He flipped the fish filets in the crackling frying pan as he spoke.

"I'm sorry to hear the policeman dragged your friend away when they thought he stole one of my sketches. My art is highly favored by the king so the police may be a little overzealous in protecting it.

Where did your friend get the picture he was showing around?" Pierre asked.

While he was busy loading the plates with toast and fish, I pulled out your sketchbook. "He drew it. He is quite a good artist himself," I told him.

We sat down at the table. Pierre was very interested in your sketchbook. I flipped it around so he could see the landscape sketch you drew.

"Not bad. May I?" Pierre asked, reaching out a hand to the sketchbook so he could see it for himself.

I didn't have a choice. (Goldie apologized to Robbie unnecessarily). I had just spent the evening invading his house and studying all of his pictures, and we needed his help. He took great care of it, making sure to wipe the table off before setting it down.

He was so engrossed in studying every picture in your sketchbook, I thought he forgot I was there. The more drawings Pierre examined, the more dumbfounded he was. He was silent, carefully studying each drawing as if in a trance. I finished eating and cleaned up the kitchen as quietly as I could. When there were no more pictures to look at, Pierre finally set the book down.

"You said his name was Robbie?" he asked. "He draws like me, but he's never studied with me. The style is unquestionably similar to mine." Knowing I probably had no idea what he was talking about, he turned the sketchbook toward me "See these long steady lines? His pencil pressure is consistent with mine. He shades like I do. It's a remarkable likeness. No wonder his art was mistaken for mine." He was definitely impressed.

Pierre took a big bite of fish, unceremoniously dumped the rest of his food in the trash, and started for the door. He said, "The jail should be open soon. Let's go get your friend. I have got to meet him."

15

MEETING PIERRE

"So where is Pierre, and how is he going to get me out?" asked Robbie anxiously, scratching unconsciously at the blistered skin on his cheek. As much as he was looking forward to getting out of jail, the thought of meeting this very esteemed, talented artist was even more exciting.

"He said he would meet us outside once he got everything straightened out," said Goldie.

Moments later a guard entered the room. It was the same guard who had unceremoniously brought Robbie to the visitation room only an hour before. This time, he acted very regal as he stood ramrod straight and announced, "You are hereby released, by order of the king."

Robbie grabbed Goldie by the hand and they went outside to meet Pierre.

"You must be Pierre." Robbie extended his hand to shake. "Thanks for getting me out of there."

With the sun in his eyes, Pierre squinted at Robbie for a minute as both males attempted to size each other up. "Hello, Robbie. It's nice to meet you. I believe this belongs to you." Pierre held out Robbie's sketchbook.

Robbie blushed hotly and retrieved his sketchbook from this man who was an artistic genius, the same one whose work he had been admiring for days. This was the man whose art inspired Elyrise the Wise. This was the man whose artwork would complete this test. Robbie would now be able return to his own home where he imagined his mother was now out of her mind with worry. This was the man who could restore his mother's happiness. This was also the man who had just seen his sketchbook—his own amateur art. One comment from Pierre could fill Robbie with pride or cut him to the quick. Robbie was unable to look Pierre in the eye as he awaited Pierre's assessment.

Pierre was an astute man who was watching Robbie carefully and noticed the flurry of emotions cross his face in just those few seconds and quickly ended Robbie's anxiety. "It's good—very good. In fact, the King was impressed. He wants to meet you."

"The King wants to meet me!" Robbie squeaked. Clearing his throat, he tried again. "Why does he want to meet me? And how did you convince him to let me out?" Robbie was scratching at his face and arms as he spoke.

"It's a long story. You must be starved. I know I am. Let's talk over lunch," Pierre said as he led the way. He strolled to a nearby stream and stooped to pull some weeds. While Robbie watched Pierre's odd behavior, he asked Goldie hopefully if she had found his art case back at the marketplace.

"It's safe," she said just as Pierre came back to Robbie and handed him the weeds.

"Gee, thanks? You don't have to give me any...flowers. I should be thanking you for getting me out of that jail." Robbie said confused by the strange gift.

"This plant is jewelweed and an antidote for poison sumac. Smear the leaves all over your rash and the itching will go away," explained Pierre.

Not wanting to offend the man who had just rescued him and whom he still needed, Robbie did as he was told. He instantly felt a cooling sensation as the juice from the plant dried on his face and arms. Sure enough, his itchy skin became a little more bearable.

"Save this for later," Pierre said, handing him some more. "You will want to reapply it a couple more times today until your itching stops for good."

Pierre bent down once again and held some of the weeds in the stream, "If you ever need more, just look for the leaves that shine like silver underwater."

Robbie studied the silver leaves Pierre held in the stream then tucked the rest of the jewelweed in his pocket.

They crossed the street to enter a cozy little bistro. Once they had ordered their lunch, Pierre told them about his morning.

"After I sent Goldie to visit you, I went to New Camelot to see the King. King Arthur was getting ready to fly over the majestic mountains. He had gotten wind of a fight brewing between the Mountain People and the inhabitants of the Lake District--some kind of boundary dispute."

Pierre paused, noticing Robbie's mouth was open in surprise. Pierre raised a questioning eyebrow.

"Would that be King Arthur of Camelot?" Robbie asked, "I love those stories."

"Well, New Camelot, but yes, it is the *inpilqued* King Arthur," explained Pierre, assuming, of course, that Robbie was a native of the

LOL and familiar with the *inpilquing* process. "He spends most of his spare time at 'New Camelot'. Not very original if you ask me."

Anyway, I caught King Arthur just as he was leaving. He granted me a visit, hoping to learn I'd finished the latest painting he had commissioned. Instead, I showed him some of your sketches. He was angry when he thought my painting was still only a sketch until I explained to him that these were the sketches of a teenage boy. Robbie, he was very intrigued by your work. When I told him what happened at the marketplace, he was only too eager to write a pardon to get you out of jail. There is one condition: I am to bring you to meet him tomorrow."

"Me?" Robbie croaked. Again, he cleared his throat, "Let me get this straight, *King Arthur* wants to meet me in *New Camelot* tomorrow?"

"That's correct. New Camelot is a bit different from the *inpilqued* Camelot which he must visit regularly. In New Camelot, he doesn't want to make the same mistakes. He still uses a round table, but his chair sits a bit higher than the other eleven less the knights forget that their loyalty is to him. He refuses to love a woman, but has chosen to love only art, for it cannot break his heart. He has developed a passion for my art and has commissioned me to paint many pieces for him." Pierre's voice rang hollow, which was surprising for someone who must be highly favored by the King.

"Well, that's wonderful, isn't it?" asked Goldie.

"King Arthur hasn't changed as much as he thinks. He still takes what he wants from whomever he wants without considering their needs. He pays me well but expects much. I don't need his money. I would prefer the freedom to paint whatever I wanted and go wherever I wanted. His demands keep me on a short leash."

"What would happen if you refused?" asked Goldie.

"I'm afraid to find out. He has long insisted that I live at New Camelot, available to him at his whim, but I have persuaded him to let me live in my cabin and do my work there. If I upset him, I'm afraid he will change his mind."

"You mean, he would keep you a prisoner?" Goldie was horrified by this possibility.

Pierre merely shrugged, "I don't want to find out."

"How long have you been painting for him? You can't be more than twenty-five years old?" commented Robbie.

"You have obviously not been in the Human's Hills for long." Pierre chuckled and gestured toward Goldilocks, "Just like Fairy Tale Town, nobody ages here. I am forty, but stopped aging when I was twenty-seven and arrived in the Human's Hills."

"I know Goldilock's story, but how about telling me yours? I am not familiar with a young artist named Robbie," inquired Pierre.

Robbie looked questioningly at Goldie, but it was his decision to make. From all that Goldie related to him this morning, he knew she trusted Pierre.

There was something that made Robbie want to trust him too, but the Human's Hills had not been kind to him. Pierre seemed different from the others, and he liked him already. Despite wanting to trust Pierre, he still felt the need to abbreviate the beginning, "I lost something in the Great Meadow of Fairy Tale Town that was important, and I can't possibly go home to my mother without it." Robbie let the implication be that he was afraid to face his mother, but his words were not actually a lie.

Robbie continued his story, "I searched all over for it, but could not find it. My friend, Little Boy Blue sent me to the Wizard to ask for a Transparency detector."

At the name of the Wizard, Pierre made a slight choking sound. Robbie paused, uncertain, but Pierre gestured for him to continue.

"Well, the Wizard gave me only a riddle and asked for one thousand dollars to borrow a Transparency detector. Little Boy Blue and my other friends, thought we might pick the cash at the Forest of Money, but when we got there, Elyrise the Wise gave me another riddle which led me here to obtain a treasure from you."

At Elyrise's name, Pierre again choked.

This time, Robbie asked him to explain himself.

"Sorry, it's nothing bad. It's only that I met the Wizard and Elyrise myself a number of years ago when I had a very unfortunate accident.

Both are very wise, but neither were able to help me. The Wizard has a twisted sense of humor and makes people work hard to discover what is right under their noses. Elyrise is a friend of mine, but likes to test people to their limits. He believes that only through hard work can someone truly be satisfied."

"What were their riddles?" asked Pierre

Robbie recited them quickly from memory, first the Wizard's:

"Thine eyes have I seen once with mine.

A pair of two over this time.

Over the Human's Hills, below a peak,

There you will find what most you seek."

Then he recited Elyrise's:

"Over the hills through the In Betweenz

You will discover what this task means.

Find answers long sought out

And bring back a treasure beyond a doubt."

Yes, I remember those from your sketch book." Pierre said as he stared into Robbie's unusual colored eyes. An odd look crossed his face.

"Any idea what the riddles mean?" he questioned.

"I haven't got a clue. Now, I'm so far from home, and can't return until I get a Transparency Detector. I can't imagine what my mother is thinking?"

"What about your father? Did you ask him to help you?" Pierre asked.

"My father is gone." Robbie said it in a tone that made Pierre drop that line of questioning.

"I'm sorry," Pierre apologized. Pierre still didn't recognize any part of Robbie's story that was *inpilqued*, but decided that too was Robbie's decision to share when he was ready.

Robbie started scratching again, and Pierre reminded him to re-apply the jewelweed.

"If those are the clothes you were wearing in the poison sumac patch, you'd better change. The oil from the poison is likely still on your clothes," Pierre said as he realized that neither of them had any luggage with them.

Pierre stood up and dropped some money on the table, "We'd better get a few things for tomorrow."

Pierre bought new outfits for the children that were suitable for meeting the King without being overly fancy. Robbie was very grateful for the blue trousers, the green velvet jacket with the plumed sleeves, the white linen shirt and the very comfortable new shoes. He hastily threw his school uniform in the trash deciding it was not salvageable after the adventures of the last few days. Goldie did the same with her torn and tattered clothes assuring her companions that she had dozens of Goldilocks' outfits. She was thrilled with her beautiful new gown of deep purple and her matching shoes. Not wanting to mess up their new garments, Pierre bought them something casual and comfortable to wear back to his home.

With the shopping done, Pierre glanced at his watch. Robbie noticed this timeless gesture and found it curious, since no one else he'd met in the Land of Legends even wore a watch. Blue had told him, time was irrelevant, and what you needed to know you could glean from the position of the sun in the sky.

"We'd better get going," Pierre suddenly seemed anxious to get back to his cabin.

As they hiked back to the cabin, Robbie asked Pierre about the legendary people that lived in the Human's Hills. Pierre told him he had met Hercules, Paul Bunyan, and Davy Crocket. He'd also met Martin Luther King, Babe Ruth and even Elvis Presley. One time, he even met Mother Theresa.

"But some of those are real people who died. How did they end up here? Do their histories get *inpilqued* like fairy tales?" Robbie wanted to know.

"Yes and no. *Inpilquing* is only for fictional characters," Pierre explained. "Non fictional characters whose histories are legendary get *abpilqued* and become immortal beings in the Land of Legends."

"But what about saintly people like Mother Theresa? Does she have a choice? Doesn't she get to go to heaven?" Robbie was not sure *abpilquing* was all that desirable if one spent his or her whole life striving to get to heaven.

"Only souls ascend to heaven when people die. If a person destined for heaven is *abpilqued*, their soul is duplicated when they die and their original soul ascends to heaven. Their duplicated soul remains in their *abpilqued* bodies which resemble the age they were when they became legendary."

"Why haven't I seen any of these legendary people?" asked Robbie.

"The Land of Legends is a big place, you have seen only a portion of the Human's Hills. The common people you have met were important in some legend's history, you just don't remember them."

For the first time, Robbie wished he could hang around the Human's Hills a bit longer to meet some of these guys.

As they climbed the hill leading to the cabin, Robbie looked way up and the view of the waterfall took his breath away as he recognized the scene from Pierre's landscape painting.

It was almost dark by the time they got to the cabin. Pierre flipped the switch inside the door and the portraits lining the walls sprang to life. The portraits closest to the door were of a boy next to one of a girl in their early teens. "These are good. Amazing, actually!" Robbie exclaimed. "Your portraits really *are* as fantastic as your landscapes."

Robbie examined the rows of children's portraits hung in decreasing age order. There were similarities among some of the children, and some of the pictures bore a resemblance to Pierre, "Are these relatives of yours? Do you have children?" asked Robbie.

The mask hiding Pierre's sorrow threatened to crack, "I have one child—lives with the mother. I have never actually seen the child, but that doesn't stop me from wondering. Each year, I paint portraits of children in town and hang them up as if I was hanging my own child's picture."

"Do you have a son or a daughter?" Goldie asked.

Pierre checked his watch again and failed to answer Goldie. He moved quickly to the other side of the room where he turned on the Omniview and began flipping through the channels.

Goldie whispered to Robbie, "That's an Omniview. He must be well commissioned by the King since few private citizens can afford to own one of these. They have thousands of channels and can access cities all over the galaxy. You can even set it to tune into cities at different periods of history."

Robbie stared in awe as familiar and unfamiliar landscapes flashed by. He was certain he spotted some alien creatures as Pierre soared through the channels.

Suddenly, Pierre stopped, having found the channel he sought. He sat on the edge of his lounge chair, oblivious to his guests as he stared at the screen.

Robbie and Goldie were too curious about Pierre's behavior to do anything other than observe. Goldie pulled up a chair. Robbie was too amazed to sit as he stared at the Omniview. He moved closer and closer to the screen in open-mouthed wonder as the camera slowly zoomed in, and Robbie realized from the familiar buildings that it was not just from his own world, it was his own Rosecrest City. He silently named the landmarks to himself until the camera focused on one of the theaters. It was his mother's theater. As the camera magically passed through the roof of the building, the audio kicked in. Robbie could hear the pre-performance chatter from the audience; it was interrupted by an announcement. "The part of Mrs. Darling will be played by the understudy, Anne Marie Harlin."

That was his mother's part!

"No! Not again. Something's wrong, I know it," Pierre ranted as he ran his fingers through his hair in anger and frustration. Robbie was used to his mother having fans, but shocked that her fame would have reached the LOL. He was even more shocked by such a strong reaction from Pierre who had been so kind and even-tempered until now.

Robbie didn't want to stare at Pierre and something past Pierre's head caught Robbie's attention. The wall he was now facing was also full of paintings, only most of these were scenes as Goldilocks had described. He was very familiar with these scenes. They were fairy tales like the ones his mother starred in her plays. He turned on a light to view these better. He couldn't believe it, *these actually were the plays his mother starred in, and there was his mother in each scene! Pierre was a very big fan.*

Robbie saw a lone portrait mixed in with the fairy tale scenes. It was a portrait of his mother! He reached out and grabbed it off the wall, "That is my..."

Pierre had jumped out of his seat when Robbie removed the portrait, yelling at the same time, "That is my..."

"...mother!" finished Robbie.

"...wife!" Pierre finished simultaneously.

"What?" they both asked at the same time as they stared wide-eyed at each other. Robbie's lavender eyes had turned silver with emotion as he stared into another set of silver eyes.

Pierre repeated himself, "That is my wife."

Robbie said, "That's not possible. My mother was married to Sebastian Sartes. My father ran off and deserted my mother right before I was born."

Pierre's legs gave out and he sat down hard on the chair, holding his head in his hands in misery. After a moment, he asked, "Did she tell you that? Does she really believe that?"

Robbie just stared at this man who was claiming his mother.

"Sebastian," Pierre said, recalling a cherished memory. "She always called me that. Gabrielle was my 'Belle' and I was her 'Sebastian.' You know? From *Beauty and the Beast*?"

Then he drew the rest of the conclusion, "You," Pierre faltered momentarily, "must be my son." He finished in a choked voice.

Pierre looked at Robbie who was now scowling at him with all the anger a boy, who thought he too had been deserted, would feel.

Goldie moved in closer to Robbie, wanting to offer support by her presence. She said nothing--this was Robbie's moment—Robbie's and his father's.

Pierre looked down for a moment and noticed the hard object that his foot had just kicked. A partially concealed wooden box was lying next to his favorite chair, but he hadn't noticed it until now.

"My art case!" Robbie and Pierre exclaimed in unison, surprised by the unexpected appearance of an object that had been equally treasured by both of them.

Pierre slowly reached down and his finger lovingly traced the wood carving of the lion's tale on the top of the box. He wanted to jump up and embrace the boy, but could see the anger and resentment on Robbie's face and thought he better proceed carefully. "This box was given to me by an eccentric man in an antique shop when I was a young man of twenty. I loved it and took it everywhere, that is, until my whole world was torn in half and I was irrevocably separated from my beloved wife and our unborn child." Pierre's voice was full of emotion and there were tears in his eyes.

Robbie said nothing as the conflicting emotions fought to sort themselves out in his own head.

Pierre lifted the box onto his lap and the invisible backpack that had been concealing it fell to the floor with a soft "thunk." When Pierre looked at the spot, he saw nothing and he gave Robbie a queer look. He reached out and felt for the invisible backpack. "So, you found it then?" Pierre asked as he flipped the box around and opened the secret compartment where the glitter crayon was kept hidden.

Robbie reached down and slowly pulled the crayon out of the box. He held it out in front of him like a peace offering, acknowledging the crayon's original owner.

Pierre slid the art case out of his lap and stood up in one fluid motion, wrapping his arms around Robbie. Robbie hugged him tightly back, tears streaming down both faces.

Goldie quietly took a few steps backward, easing herself into a chair, silent tears rolling past the wide smile on her face.

16

PIERRE'S STORY

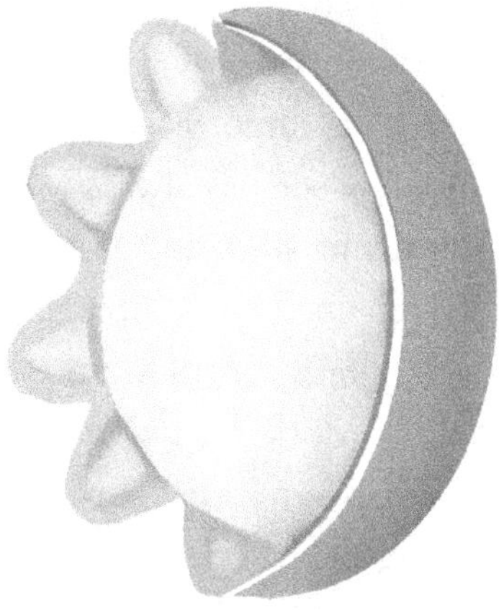

Goldie wanted to give father and son a chance to get acquainted, so she suggested they sit outside in the backyard while she made something for them to eat.

They settled into comfortable Adirondack chairs and Pierre made them a cozy fire in the outdoor brick fireplace.

"Why did Belle, I mean, your mother, tell you that I had abandoned her and you? She doesn't really believe that? Surely, she remembers the terror of that night?" Pierre trailed off.

"Actually, she doesn't remember it at all." Robbie started to explain.

His mother never wanted him to talk about her private life with anyone—so many secrets—but he thought if anyone had a right to know, it was his father. "Thirteen and a half years ago, on the morning of October 26th, my mother woke up at the hospital bruised and battered and was handed a newborn baby. She remembers nothing about the night before. She was found unconscious in Hopler Park and was brought to the hospital. One of the nurses recognized her from *Beauty and the Beast* and called the theater. You could not be found so her agent, Rosalie, now my Godmother was called and has helped her put herself and her career back together.

"You might as well know, it hasn't been easy for her, for us." Robbie said somewhat accusatory.

"She suffered an injury to her brain that night and still has not gotten her memory back completely. Since the accident, she has difficulty adding new things to her memory. If it weren't for Rosalie's help those first few years, she might have forgotten she had a baby. She forgot my name a lot, but fortunately she has always loved the name Robbie. Every time she forgot my name, she said, 'I think I'll call you Robbie after my grandfather'. She renamed me Robbie dozens of times.

"Names, words, conversations, scripts were especially hard for her to remember. Mom couldn't work for a long time. Her money was running out. Then Rosalie discovered that her memory from before the accident was impeccable. Rosalie had her auditioning for parts in plays she already knew like *Beauty and the Beast*, and *Peter Pan*. Fortunately, mom was such a fan of theater growing up that she had memorized entire screenplays with everyone's parts."

"I watch her in every play on the Omniview. She is still young, still talented and still beautiful," Pierre said worshipfully. His voice was thick with emotion, and he had been listening to Robbie's story without interrupting.

Just then, Goldie brought out some sandwiches. They wanted her to join them, but Goldie pleaded exhaustion and left them alone once again.

Robbie continued, "Although mom tries to maintain her star image in public, nobody knows we live a no-frills lifestyle in a tiny one-bedroom rowhouse on the corner of Hopler Park." Robbie stopped to swat at the mosquitoes that had come out when Goldie brought out the sandwiches and a lantern. The mosquitoes only made his already itchy skin worse.

The mention of Hopler Park flooded Pierre with memories, but he noticed his son's discomfort and stood up, "Let me make us a tent. There is still so much to say. I love sleeping outside. Do you mind?"

Robbie shook his head.

"Good. The cabin is small, and this way we won't keep Goldie up all night." Pierre pulled something out of his pocket and started to draw. It looked like Robbie's glitter crayon and Robbie reached inside his pocket. His was still in his pocket where he had tucked it after their emotional reunion. *So, there must be two.*

"Did you forget?" Robbie asked incredulously. "It doesn't work after dark."

Pierre smiled as he continued to draw, "Yours doesn't. You have 'Sundust.' This is 'Moonbeam.' Mine doesn't work in the daytime. I had it in my pocket that fateful night when I left 'The World Out There'."

Robbie reached out and felt the tent. Pierre worked quickly, impressing Robbie with how fast he could draw. In a few minutes, it was finished, complete with a zipper. Robbie swatted at another mosquito.

"Here, take the light in. The moon is all I need. Let me just make the cots and I'll be right in," said Pierre.

They got comfortably settled on their cots complete with pillows and blankets which Pierre retrieved from the cabin as they were more comfortable than the invisible ones could be. Pierre asked, "You said you live on the edge of Hopler Park? Belle always loved that park, especially the romantic old cemetery. We began dating when she was starring in *Beauty in the Beast*. She played Belle, of course, and I was the set designer. She was very young and very beautiful. I don't know what she saw in me; I was poor and penniless, but we fell in love. Her very proper parents didn't approve of our relationship so we would meet secretly at Hopler Park on the edge of the city. Tragically, her parents were killed in a car accident and she was left all alone. She was only 18 and had no other relatives. We were in love and I wanted to take care of her—so we got married. I was seven years older and I had been living on my own for a while. We were so happy, and a few months later she told me we were having a baby.

"She was starring in *Sleeping Beauty* at the time. She was strong. The costumes concealed her stomach and she chose to keep working until she was seven months pregnant. She was happy in the theater. We had the perfect life. Then, on October 25th, Belle couldn't sleep. She wanted to walk around Hopler Park, so I indulged her. She wasn't afraid of the little cemetery and thought that it was such a romantic old place, so we went in there. Belle had learned the life stories of most of the people buried there. We noticed right away that Julian Smythe's grave was open. open casket was empty. Julian was the youngest and longest surviving son of the wealthy landowner whose plantation later became Rosecrest City. While Julian's father Jeremy was well-loved during his life, Julian was greedy and sold his father's land. The money brought him only tragedy. It was rumored that his wife, his only heir, buried the cursed money with him when he died. That night, Julian's grave had been disturbed. We looked in the hole, but it was too dark to see anything. We didn't realize that whoever had robbed this grave was coming back, then we heard the grave robbers returning to the dark cemetery. We were trapped and needed a place to hide. I tucked Belle into the shadows on the other side of the mausoleum, half hidden by a tree.

"The space wasn't large enough for me to hide next to her. I had little time. I hid inside the scoop of a tractor and drew a board to cover myself. I drew a doorknob so I'd have a handle to hold it in place. There was a soft pile of dirt underneath me, which I sunk into so it supported my invisible board snugly over me.

"I should have connected the tractor to the grave robbery, but I didn't. To my horror, one of the grave robbers came directly over to the tractor and dumped the dirt into the grave, along with me and my board. I prayed it was too dark for Belle to see me, because I'm sure she would have screamed and we both would have been killed. It was a hard landing, but fortunately I kept hold of my board as I fell. I realized the gravity of my mistake and decided I had to face the grave robbers or be buried alive. I used the handle to push on the door, planning to stand up and reveal myself."

Robbie gasped, knowing before Pierre finished, exactly how his father had ended up in the Land of Legends. He had literally been sitting on the edge of his seat for this part of the story. He had not said a word while Pierre told the story of the night he was born, noting the parallels to his own experiences in the same graveyard.

Robbie burst out, "You opened an invisible door to the Land of Legends," finishing Pierre's story. He then quickly told Pierre the beginning of his own story, which he had previously omitted.

Then Robbie asked, "But, why didn't you ever come back to us? Does this place mean more to you then we do?"

"Oh no! Robbie, you must believe me!" Pierre pleaded desperately and grabbed Robbie's hand "I tried and tried to come back to you, I still try, but my door is still buried in a grave below a few feet of dirt. Do you know they don't have dynamite in the LOL, or bombs? If only I had armed myself with more useful skills than creating art, or a tool other than a crayon, maybe I could have made my own bomb.

"I draw new doors all the time trying to draw my way back home. Every time I opened an invisible door, I ended up in a different place. I've gotten a glimpse of a lot of different places, but have not seen anything resembling Earth during this century. I've never stepped more than two feet into these new worlds, afraid to let the door shut behind me. Not even the Wizard can explain exactly how these crayons work and he was the eccentric man who sold it to me."

"But wait," Robbie interrupted excitedly. "How did the Wizard get to Rosecrest City to sell you the art case in the first place?"

"Ahh, the Wizard is actually a 'mad scientist' from our world. He invented two sets of crayons and discovered their magical ability to create invisible objects into existence. Just like you and me, he drew himself into the Land of Legends. He went back and forth many times keeping the secret to himself. He discovered the secret to immortality in the LOL, figured out how to get himself *inpilqued* by writing his own story and making it famous. He sold the other set of crayons to me. I recognized him during one of my visits to Fairy Tale Town, and confronted him. He was apologetic and could not help me, but he assured me that he destroyed the formula for the crayons so no one else would face the same tragedy."

"So, do you think I will be able to get back home? I know mom must be awfully worried. It's been five days." Robbie said.

Pierre thought for a moment. "Your mother is definitely worried about you. That is why she has missed all of her performances this week. We have to find your door and get back to her."

"I sure hope you have a better way of traveling to Fairy Tale Town than passing through the In Betweenz." Robbie shuddered, but merely said, "I can't make Goldie go through there again."

Pierre said gently, "Get some sleep. I'll take care of everything in the morning." Robbie lay down and Pierre pulled the blanket up over him, affectionately smoothing his hair before settling onto his own cot only a few feet away from the thirteen-year-old son he had just met.

17

NEW CAMELOT

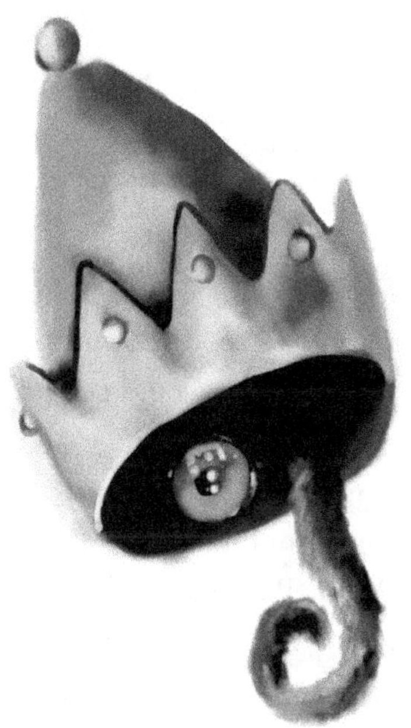

"Did you two have a nice talk last night?" asked Goldie as they sat down to eat breakfast, which Pierre had whipped up for the three of them.

Robbie gave her the quick version of how Pierre had come to the LOL and why he had not been able to return.

Goldie clasped her hands together in excitement and exclaimed, "When we find Robbie's door, you will both be able to return!"

"That's right!" said Robbie. Pierre said nothing and nodded his head, but not before Goldie saw the look of concern briefly cross his face, then disappear behind the mask he once again put on. Robbie was sitting next to Pierre and had not seen it so Goldie chose not to comment. Anxious to be on their way, Robbie asked, "How far is it to New Camelot?"

"The waterfall begins at the feet of the sleeping giant you see on that mountain range," Pierre pointed to the rock formation behind them which indeed looked like the big feet of a reclining giant stretching off into the distance the length of his legs, torso and finally his head. "Behind the mountain, below the head of the sleeping giant, lies New Camelot."

The mountain was steep, "Are you saying we have to *climb* over that mountain? It looks like pretty rough going." Robbie's hopes of getting home before the end of the day were crushed.

"Not to worry," Pierre assured him. "We could walk along the mountain the entire length of the sleeping giant's body, and around his head, and enter New Camelot from that direction, but that is not an easy trail. That is the way most travelers would go and it would take hours, but I have a secret short cut. As I told you, the king has me on a short leash and wants easy access to my cabin. More importantly, he wants me to come quickly when he summons me."

After breakfast was over, Pierre stirred the embers that remained in the fireplace from the night before. As Robbie held back the flaps, Pierre emptied the contents of the invisible tent, then balled up the tent and tossed it in the fireplace. Robbie watched as the flames surrounded the tent giving some shape to that which was invisible. Pierre broke the cots and added those as well.

"Why did you do that?" Robbie asked. He had not destroyed anything that he had drawn.

"After years of tripping over the invisible objects that piled up and could not be seen, I learned burning them when I finished with them was the easiest way to dispose of them."

The fire had nearly burned itself out before Pierre was done talking, the invisible items burned as quickly as a piece of paper.

Goldie emerged from the cabin wearing her dress of purple, the color of royalty. Robbie caught a glance of her out of the corner or his eye, then looked up for a second, much longer glance. The purple of the dress brought out the color in her cheeks. She had showered and pulled her hair up on the top of her head which showed off her long graceful neck. The neck of the dress was scooped, making her seem older than when she wore her traditional frock with its ruffle around the collar. Robbie looked into her blue eyes that shone brightly like jewels, then he blushed deeply when he realized she was watching him looking at her.

"Well, what do you think?" Goldilocks said as she lifted the hem of her skirt and twirled daintily around.

Robbie swallowed hard, realizing not for the first time, how stunningly beautiful his companion was. "Um, nice," he said.

Goldie blushed too, not minding his understated comment, but gaining much more satisfaction from his unspoken reaction.

"You look nice too," she said, acknowledging Robbie's new clothes.

Ignoring the teenage awkwardness in the room, Pierre grabbed a brown bag from the refrigerator, and a lantern, and announced it was time to go.

Robbie hoisted the invisible backpack and grabbed his art case. He tossed out the empty bag from Elyrise. Goldie still had the coin purse in her pocket.

"What's that?" Robbie asked Pierre about the brown bag.

"Oh, just a snack," said Pierre casually and he headed off toward the waterfall.

The trio followed a bubbling stream, leading them to the powerful waterfall they could now hear. Goldie spotted the plant from the day before growing alongside the stream. Careful not to mess up her dress, she picked some and tested it in the water, holding it under so they could see the shimmering silver of its "jeweled" leaves. She handed it to Robbie who enthusiastically rubbed it on his still irritated, though much improved, skin.

The trail was easy going, even in their dress clothes and nice shoes. They approached an alcove, where the high rock walls had been smoothly eroded by the continuous trickle of water on either side of the graceful waterfall. The noise of the waterfall, cascading over a rock jutting out at center stage, blocked out all other sound. At the bottom of the enchanting waterfall, was a crystal clear pool rippling out from the base of the falls. They had come upon the source of the stream they had been following and saw several other streams branching off of this pool, one flowing towards the sleeping giant's head and the other, larger stream, heading straight down the mountain with further dips, twists and plunges.

Pierre stopped at the pool and cupped his hands to drink from the cool water. Robbie bent to do the same, then held his cupped hands out to Goldie so she didn't have to kneel down in her pretty dress.

The noise of the waterfall made it difficult to communicate so they huddled close together so they wouldn't have to shout and disturb the peacefulness of this place.

"This is my shortcut," Pierre said, directing his gaze right into the waterfall.

Robbie, seeing nothing but a dead end with high rock walls, the waterfall, the pool and a few shrubs, said, "I hope you are not going to tell us we have to jump in and swim down to a secret cave to get past this waterfall, because, well, I'm not a swimmer."

Pierre shimmied along the rock wall on a narrow path as he skirted around the pool, passed behind a tall shrub, and disappeared from view. Robbie and Goldie were puzzled, but took off after Pierre. When they passed behind the shrub, they found a huge boulder that partially concealed a crack in the sheer face of the rock wall. The crack was barely two feet wide but extended higher than Robbie's head. They could see nothing but pitch darkness when they peered into the crack. Then they saw the light from the lantern go on and followed Pierre inside.

"Wonderful!" exclaimed Goldie, who was also relieved that they didn't have to jump into the water and ruin their beautiful new clothes.

The entrance passageway was initially narrow, but then opened up so they could walk side by side with Pierre leading the way. They zigzagged around some of the larger rock formations that growing from the cave's ceiling and its floor. Pierre explained that they were traveling underneath the form of the Sleeping Giant. The size of the cave grew as they approached its center which lay underneath the torso of the sleeping giant. Here, the cave was nearly two stories high and just as wide.

As they stood in the center of the cave, they heard a horrific noise that made Robbie and Goldie stop dead in their tracks. Goldie grabbed Robbie, clutching his hand in a vise grip. "What's that?" she whispered. They heard the noise again, sounding like something between a roar and a moan.

Pierre's pace did not falter, and he failed to notice that Robbie and Goldie had stopped. When the light from the lantern in Pierre's hand began to fade from view, leaving them in near darkness, the children called out to him.

"Don't let the noise scare you. That's just 'the Beast.' We're old friends. I think he knows I'm near." Pierre kept walking as he spoke, and the noise of the Beast grew increasingly louder.

"Just stay behind me and show no fear," advised Pierre as they veered around a large grouping of rock formations and came face to face with an enormous dragon. His scales were the color of golden topaz and shimmered in the dim light of the lantern. He stood directly in the center of the passageway, his head nearly touching the ceiling. He was staring at Pierre in anticipation, and Pierre slowly approached the dragon.

Robbie and Goldie were certain he was anticipating his next meal, which in fact, he was. Pierre needn't have worried about Robbie and Goldie staying behind him. They stayed rooted to the spot as he called to the Beast, "Hey Boy, I brought you something," Pierre held up the bag he had brought. The dragon lifted his great big head, gave it a mighty shake and let out another roar.

Then the Beast dipped his head and sniffed at the bag. Pierre spoke loudly to the dragon. "Say please."

In jaw dropping amazement, Robbie and Goldie watched the dragon extend one scaly leg and dipped his head behind the outstretched leg, in a gesture that resembled a courtly bow.

"Good boy," Pierre said as he withdrew from the bag, a very large raw steak. In deference to his guests, Pierre threw the steak to the side of the widest part of the passageway to distract the Beast, and to allow Robbie and Goldie to slip quietly by the occupied dragon, without getting too close to it.

Once out of earshot, Robbie asked about the dragon in the cave.

"He is at the King's disposal. The cave makes a large, natural cage. He can't get out on my end, because the passageway is too small. The King has a large gate at the entrance of the cave. If anybody found the hidden entranceway at the waterfall, encountering the dragon would make them turn around and run out of the cave. The 'Beast" is better than having a guarded fence. So, the shortcut to the King's stays a secret."

"How is it that you and the Beast have become such good friends?" asked Robbie.

Pierre explained, "On rare occasions, the King lets me borrow the dragon to visit Fairy Tale Town. It's one of the only forms of air travel they have here in the LOL. You might have noticed, they don't build anything that pollutes the air, like cars, trains or airplanes."

"I haven't noticed any other dragons, is there another way of traveling?" Robbie was hopeful there was a faster way for him to return home than walking, but he would prefer not to get any closer to a monstrous dragon.

Pierre said, "You're right, dragons are very rare. Most people do not travel between the lands. They live exactly where they have always lived, Fairy Tales live near Fairy Tale Town, heroes live in the Human Hills, the Mountain People live in the Mountains, etc. I don't really belong anywhere, which is why I'm more restless than most. My door opened right into the center of Fairy Tale Town, so I must visit it often. Of course, I am not a Fairy Tale so I feel I blend in better with the people of the Human's Hills.

The whole walk from Pierre's cabin was little more than a mile over fairly easy, if dark, terrain. In no time at all, Robbie and Goldie saw that the mouth of the cave did, indeed, end at a huge gate. Cut into the dragon-sized gate was a small human-sized door with a spring latch on the exterior side.

"What now?" asked Goldie.

Pierre shrugged and stuck his arm through the iron slats of the door and popped the spring latch. "The Beast can't do that," he said as he held up his human size arm and wiggled his slender fingers by way of explanation.

"No, but your arm is *just right*," Goldilocks giggled, joyful to be leaving the cave and the dragon behind.

The castle gates opened as the trio approached. There arrival had been expected. The King's emissary led them into the Grand Foyer of the castle and bade them wait while he announced them to the King.

The Grand Foyer was a grandiose room nearly four stories high with a painting on the ceiling resembling Michelangelo's masterpiece on the ceiling of the Sistine chapel. The floor was made of green Italian marble. At the opposite end of the room was an ornate marble wall with a balcony above it. There were two sets of curved marble stairs leading up to the balcony, one on either side of the room.

"King Arthur will see you now. You may follow me," announced the Emissary. They hadn't even seen him return. He was a short man dressed in a green silk outfit with puffy sleeves and short baggy pants that cuffed above the knees. Green tights, pointy gold satin shoes and a tall gold hat with multiple points completed his ensemble. Robbie and Goldie thought the hat was unusual, particularly when it shifted around of its own accord.

The emissary led them up one of the marble staircases. Pierre smiled to himself but remained silent as if he was enjoying an inside joke as he followed the group up the steps. From the top, the balcony overlooked the entrance door on one side and a ballroom on the other side. The ballroom was bigger than the gymnasium at Robbie's school! This floor was hardwood, but different types of wood and wood stains were used on the floorboards to create elaborate designs on the floor. Colorful pillars lined both sides of the room and held up the balcony that encircled the ballroom ending in a winding staircase on the far end of the ballroom which divided into dual spirals.

The emissary led them down one of the balconies through a set of double doors leading to a long hallway with portraits along both sides. Passing through another set of double doors at the end of the hallway, they entered a three-story glass solarium that sounded like a jungle. Robbie was following behind the emissary, and saw a large eyeball peeking out from the brim of the hat, before the brim slipped back into place. Half a dozen live trees were planted around the room--banana trees, palm trees and fragrant flowering trees. Tall tropical plants with bright flowers in all the colors of the rainbow grew amongst the trees. Butterflies and colorful birds flew around the trees, the birds chirping merrily.

"Giving them the nickel tour, huh Burt?" said Pierre sarcastically. The emissary briefly winked at Pierre before resuming his serious expression. At that moment, a parrot flew down and grabbed one of the points of Burt's hat flying off with it as it called "Ernie's hat, Ernie's hat".

"That's Ernie's hat. Give me back Ernie's hat." Burt yelled at the bird as he jumped at the hat, and the little monkey that was hanging from it grasping the brim tightly with its tiny little fists.

Pierre reacted quickly and grabbed the little monkey as the bird flew over his head. Losing interest in the gold hat once its inhabitant was gone, the parrot released it from its beak. The hat fell into the shrubs on the ground.

Burt hustled down the wrought iron spiral staircase that was in the center of the room. The group followed closely behind him, Pierre cradling Ernie in his arms. Burt briefly left the path to retrieve his hat. He returned it to his head. Ernie leapt from Pierre's arms to Burt's then jumped to Burt's shoulders and crawled back under the gold hat.

On the far side of the solarium, Burt led them out of the solarium into a large library on the bottom floor, but not before they spotted the Olympic-sized swimming pool through the glass walls of the solarium. Passing through the library, they peered in an open doorway to a spacious dining room with a table that looked like it could seat 100 people. They exited the library through double doors that led to a large parlor.

Once in the parlor, Robbie noticed a door that had been left slightly open. Surprisingly, he thought he recognized the entrance foyer through the crack in the door. Before he could decide if it was the room they had started in, Burt moved in front of him, blocking his view as he discreetly closed the door. They were then ushered into a hallway off of the parlor. The emissary knocked on a very large door.

18

AT THE KING'S COMMAND

"Enter." The command was issued in a rich, resonant voice communicating both authority and power.

The emissary ushered them into the King's personal parlor which was smaller but more lavish than the one they had just passed through. King Arthur was standing by the window peering out at the castle's entrance. Despite the ordinary pose, there was no mistaking him for an average man. Even without a crown on his head, his regal posture and expensive looking robes announced he was a wealthy and powerful man.

"Good day to you, Pierre," the King addressed his friend.

Pierre bowed. "Your Highness. May I present to you, Robbie, the young artist whose sketchbook you viewed yesterday?" Robbie wondered why Pierre had not said Robbie's last name or told the King he was Pierre's son, but he said nothing as he mimicked Pierre's courtly bow.

"This is his friend, Goldilocks," continued Pierre.

Goldilocks dipped into a graceful curtsy and said, "It is an honor to meet you, Your Highness."

The King acknowledged Goldie with a slight nod of his head, but greeted Robbie more enthusiastically. "Robbie, I'm sorry for your recent difficulties here in the Human's Hills. I'm glad I was able to clear up any misunderstandings."

Robbie bowed again, "Yes, Your Highness; thank you, Your Highness." Robbie continued to bow as he spoke, unfamiliar with castle protocol and not knowing when it was okay to stop.

"Please, have a seat," the King said as he gestured to the tapestried chairs in this smaller parlor.

Robbie was relieved. If it was okay to sit down, then it must be okay to stop bowing.

"Young man, I'm very impressed with your artwork," the King said to Robbie. "As you probably know by now, I am an enthusiastic collector of Pierre's artwork. I have not met anyone else that inspired me this much, until now. The drawings in your sketchbook indicate raw talent. Your replication of Pierre's art was surprisingly good and I'm not surprised your work was mistaken for his." The King had not sat down, but now began strolling back and forth in front of them with the knuckle of one of his fingers pressed against his chin as if he was pondering an idea.

His guests remained quiet, waiting for the King to continue, "You seem to be very clever with colors. I would like you to paint something for me. I'm sure you must feel some obligation to me after I had you released from jail, but don't think that. Consider this a commission and I will pay you handsomely for your services."

Robbie paled. Although Arthur was trying to sound generous, Robbie did not miss the reminder that he owed him a debt of gratitude. He looked toward Pierre for help.

Pierre spoke, "Sorry, your Majesty. Robbie is in a hurry to leave for Fairy Tale Town, where his mother is anxiously awaiting his return. We would like to be off as soon as possible. I was hoping we could borrow some transport from you to expedite our journey."

"I'm afraid that would not be possible at this time," said the King. I have continued business in the Lake District and can't spare you any transport." The King quickly dismissed his guest's other priorities.

"Now, I'd like your opinion on something," pronounced the King. "If you'll follow me..." It wasn't exactly a question so Robbie obeyed without delay.

Pierre and Goldilocks stood up to follow as well. The King motioned for them to sit back down. "Please, stay, relax. My emissary will be here momentarily, with refreshments. You must sit and enjoy," the King said.

As if on cue, Burt arrived. He held the door open for two servants who carried in a silver tea set and a tray with scones and crumpets. Goldie wondered if Ernie was still stashed under the hat, then saw him peek out under the brim. When Burt was busy pouring the tea, Goldie broke off a piece of the crumpet and held it up to the hat. A skinny little arm grabbed the morsel and disappeared back under the hat. Goldie stifled a giggle.

The King was focused on Robbie as he walked over to a bookshelf near his desk, placed two fingers on the top of a book and tilted it on its spine. This simple action triggered something the visitors could not see, but the very large tapestry behind Arthur's desk started rolling itself up, as if by magic. A hidden entranceway was revealed.

"Cool!" Robbie said then caught himself and covered his exclamation with a more dignified cough.

Arthur led Robbie up a long spiral stairwell inside of a cylindrical shaped tower. There were six windows in a column on the East wall, marking six levels of the staircase. Glancing out the window as he climbed, Robbie could just make out a huge red ball tied to a large basket. He could see a large silver emblem painted on the ball. The emblem showed twelve knights surrounding a circle, which Robbie assumed was the King's royal seal. *This must be the King's balloon transport,"* Robbie thought.

Robbie didn't know the protocol for conversing with the King so he kept quiet as they continued the climb. King Arthur climbed at a steady pace without pausing. *He sure has a lot of energy for an old man. An old, old, old man,* Robbie thought, feeling a bit out of breath himself.

Finally, they reached the top of the staircase where there was another door. The door had no handle. The King rotated the light fixture next to the door, and the door sprang open. Six more steps revealed a hidden room at the top of the hidden stairwell, and it was awe-inspiring. It was a round room about 12 feet in diameter with a low ceiling that had been painted blue. Decorative molding on the ceiling framed a small square in the middle of the room. Centered under that was a pool, the sides of which were encrusted with jewels. The room had windows all along the walls offering a panoramic view of the castle and its grounds including three more towers the size of this one, outlining the corners of the castle. The majestic mountains added a beautiful backdrop to the castle grounds. When Robbie looked way, way down, he saw the mouth of the cave he had come through earlier this morning.

"I was thinking," the King broke the silence, "that a painting of a colorful sky with clouds and angels would be perfect on this ceiling in my royal bathhouse. What do you think, young Robbie?"

"It certainly feels like we're in the clouds, way up here," Robbie said.

"Wonderful. You will find the paints and everything you need right over there," the King said gleefully as he left the room.

"Wait! I really can't stay!" Robbie said, but the big wooden door with no doorknob had already closed. Robbie ran over to the door, but it was locked. He raised his hand to bang on the door, but knew the king was the only one who could hear him and thought the king might consider it rude.

Still, he wanted to talk this over with the king, so he whipped out the invisible crayon from its place in the art case and drew an invisible door on the existing door. When he pulled it open, he did not see the stairwell, but saw a barren waste land, dotted with frothy, boiling, steaming, foul smelling puddles. He closed the door quickly.

Only then, did he notice the curtain next to the door and the six steps leading to the round room. He pulled the curtain aside, hoping for a means of escape, but found only a small washroom with a fancy toilet and sink.

Frustrated, Robbie went to inspect the paints and supplies. *I guess he really does get what he wants. It must be nice to be king.*

The paints were set out on the top of a cabinet. Inside the cabinet, a delicious selection of food and drinks were laid out for Robbie. *Some prison. I might as well make the most of this,* Robbie said to himself as he spread Port Wine cheese over a cracker.

The sky was getting dark and Robbie had almost finished painting the clouds on the ceiling. He was just going to add some touches of azure to add more dimension to the puffy clouds in the sky, when he heard footsteps on the stairs. Someone was coming for him. He could hear footsteps ascending the stairs. He ran to the door and called out. "Hello? Hello? Could someone open this door please? I need to go home." Robbie was pleased by the clouds, but didn't know much about painting angels. It wasn't something that interested him particularly.

"Robbie, is that you?" He heard Goldie's voice. Then he heard a thud against the door, rattling it, but not opening it. "Pierre and I are trying to get you out, but it's locked."

"Try rotating the light fixture next to the door so that it is perpendicular to the door," shouted Robbie.

He heard a "creak", then a "pop" and the door sprang open. Goldie bolted in and gave him a hug. This was a habit of hers he was going to miss. The flush crept over Robbie's face and Pierre watched as his son's eyes looked like molten silver. Then Pierre came in for a hug. Robbie wasn't used to thinking of Pierre as his father yet, but it sure did feel wonderful to see him again. Pierre had similar thoughts as his own silver eyes stared back at his son.

Pierre noticed some streaks of paint on Robbie's hands and one of his cheeks. A ladder was positioned on a makeshift floor carefully placed over the pool. Clouds were beautifully painted on a small square directly over the pool outlined by decorative molding like a blue frame around a masterpiece.

Pierre was impressed by what his son had accomplished, and in such a short time, but he knew there was no time to spare. "We don't have much time. Burt finally left us alone a few moments ago when he heard a commotion in the foyer. We took that opportunity to sneak up here to find you. The King has several more projects lined up for you."

Goldie peered out the window. "The king is back. I can see the men tying the balloon down now. That must have been the commotion Burt heard."

"What's the plan?" asked Robbie.

"We sneak out there and borrow the balloon," said Pierre improvising the plan on the spur of the moment.

The trio rushed headlong back down the spiral staircase. Halfway down, they heard the unmistakable sound of footsteps ascending toward them, and froze.

"Back up the stairs," barked Pierre, a new plan formulating in his head.

When they reached the tower room, the moon was shining brightly through the windows. Pierre took out his invisible crayon and drew a massive box to block the door from the inside. Then he quickly drew a braided rope and anchored it to one of the huge wrought iron candlesticks bolted to the floor.

When he was finished, he tossed the other end out the window and asked Robbie and Goldie if they knew how to climb down a rope.

Goldie nodded and Robbie answered, "Yes, I was the fastest in my gym class."

"I'm sorry Goldie, this won't be easy for you in a dress."

"Not to worry," Goldie said as she expertly tied the skirt of her dress into two pant legs.

"The rope is very strong. I promise it will hold you." Pierre and Robbie helped Goldie out the window. She skillfully, wrapped one foot around the smooth rope and glided out of view like an acrobat. Robbie went next and scurried down like a monkey. Pierre scrambled down after Robbie.

In the moonlight, Robbie could just barely see the odd shape of Pierre's back, "Do you have my art case?"

Pierre lifted an invisible strap from around his neck and handed Robbie his art case.

They stole quietly across the yard and slipped into the basket of the now deflated balloon without alerting the guards standing sentinel along the castle wall, guarding it from outside intruders.

"Do you know how to fly this thing?" Robbie whispered to Pierre.

"Sure. The King has let me borrow it before. We're lucky to have a full moon to guide us, but we need to inflate this balloon and get off the ground before the guards spot us.

Pierre handed Robbie his invisible crayon and told him to draw a huge tarp to throw over the balloon, and hope the guards don't see it until it's too late.

Pierre motioned for Goldie to release the ties, while he turned on the burners. Robbie worked as fast as he could covering the balloon as he drew, but the balloon was huge and it was going to take awhile. The big balloon was only partially concealed when it started to inflate. Robbie got excited, but then the balloon stopped rising and started deflating.

"What's wrong?" asked Robbie.

"Bad news. The tanks are empty. We can't keep the burners lit. There is no hot air to inflate the balloon."

Sirens blared and the castle floodlights came on making it look like high noon.

"Here come the guards!" yelled Goldie.

"Run for it!" Pierre yelled. Chaos ensued as the three of them jumped out of the balloon at the same time and ran in different directions. The guards split up after them.

Robbie had jumped out the back of the basket and crawled under the invisible tarp. He folded it around his head so he could see, and ran after Goldie who was nearest to him.

Pierre looked back and saw Goldie but could not find Robbie. Then Goldie disappeared from view, and Pierre could think of only one way that could have happened. He was proud of his son for being such a quick thinker.

Pierre knew Robbie would come for him next so he took off for the cave.

At the gate, Pierre did not go through the small human door, but reached behind some vines growing down the side of the cave. The large gate sprang to life, lifting with the loud sounds of gears and pulleys.

More guards came running out of the various doors of the castle intent on discovering the source of the commotion. The guards were not the only curious ones, as the glowing amber eyes of the massive dragon became visible inside the dark cave.

Pierre greeted the dragon. He spoke soothingly to it like an old friend, and the dragon bent its legs and crouched down.

Robbie and Goldie arrived at the cave well ahead of the guards, who had run around in circles when Goldie disappeared, ignoring

Pierre altogether. They hesitated only a moment before dropping the tarp, reluctant to give up the safety of their invisibility, but knowing they must reveal themselves for Pierre.

Pierre was expecting them and told them to "grab the saddle over there and toss it on his back". Robbie and Goldie exchanged terrified glances.

Pierre's voice became a little firmer, "Now! We don't have much time."

Robbie ran to the wall and attempted to lift the huge leather saddle, but it took the combined strength of the two of them to hoist the enormous leather saddle. Timidly, the two of them approached the dragon and awkwardly managed to get the saddle at the base of the dragon's neck as Pierre talked them through it. Pierre was putting a bridle around the dragon's head, scratching him soothingly in the creases of his neck and behind the ears. Pierre commanded the dragon to shift as necessary to allow the children to tighten the cinch under the dragon's belly.

Once the saddle was tightened, the duo climbed onto the seat. Quickly, Pierre climbed up in front of Robbie and with a whistle, signaled to the dragon to take off. Recalling his brief flight on Pegasus, Robbie was glad to be secured between his father and his friend. In fact, he could hardly see around his father's broad shoulders as the dragon crawled out the front gate.

The guards had reached the mouth of the cave and were pointing spears at the passengers on the dragon. The Beast felt threatened by the spears and emitted a terrifying roar. Robbie held on for dear life as the Beast lunged towards the guards. The guards took a few steps back, but aimed their spears at the dragon, defensively now. The Beast let out another roar, followed by a blast of fire. Although not in the direct line of his fire, the uniforms of the three closest guards still caught fire and they ran away from the fire-breathing dragon, screaming, diving for the ground to roll around and put the fire out. The other guards also jumped out of range, fearful for their lives.

Robbie caught a blur of color and movement at the side of the gate and saw one of the guards lift a gun off the wall of the cave.

"Gun!" Robbie yelled.

"Hold on," Pierre yelled and kicked his heels into to the dragon's sides.

The Beast lunged forward and sprang into the air as the guard lifted the gun and fired.

Shooting pain seared through Robbie's foot. "I've been shot," he yelled to Pierre as the panic set in.

Robbie's vision and hearing began to fade as he heard Pierre say, "Hold on tight to him, Goldilocks!"

19

THE JOURNEY ENDS

Robbie opened his eyes and saw white. He had trouble focusing, but he glimpsed a tall, lithe woman with pale blond hair floating above him. His eyes felt heavy, so he closed them again. His mind hung onto that picture as he tried to figure out where he was. He remembered the pain, then the shot. As sleep reclaimed him, he decided he was in heaven and had just seen an angel.

The smell of food was heavenly. Robbie felt a warm, soft bed under him like a cloud, but nothing else. No pain in his foot. In fact, he couldn't even feel his foot. *"Yes, he had definitely died and gone to*

heaven," he decided. Slowly, he opened his eyes. That same angelic face was there only this time he recognized her. The angel was Elyria from the house of Elyrise. She smiled at him, then Robbie felt a squeeze on his hand and saw Pierre holding his hand. His last few days flashed through his mind and he remembered this wasn't only a talented artist holding his hand, it was his father! Robbie decided heaven truly is a wonderful place.

"Welcome back, Sleepyhead." Pierre said, relieved that Robbie was finally waking up.

"Sleepyhead?" Robbie slurred groggily.

"Yes, you took a dragon-sized tranquilizer in your foot. You've been sleeping for hours and your foot might take a few more before its back to normal,"

"You mean I'm not dead?"

Pierre smiled at his son.

"Where's the dragon now?" asked Robbie.

"The cave is the dragon's lair. Once we dismounted and released him, he would naturally return to the lair," Pierre explained.

Thinking of his son's comfort, Pierre gestured to a pot with steam rising from it, "Elyrisia made you something to eat. Would you like to try some food—maybe soup?"

Robbie was drawn to the wonderful smells. There were piles of food on plates all around the room. Elyrisia had made chicken noodle soup, spaghetti and meatballs, French fries, jello and apple pie. Robbie accepted the bowl of soup from Pierre. Despite the growl in his stomach, his first concern was for his mother. "Pierre, I mean, Dad, I really..."

Just then, Elyrise walked into the room. Robbie was happy to see him, and then he panicked. Robbie hadn't completed his quest, he had not brought back a new painting. Robbie was pretty sure his father would paint him one, but how long would that take? He needed to get home.

"Congratulations, my boy!" Elyrise smiled and handed Robbie a satchel.

Setting the soup aside, Robbie peeked in the satchel and saw ten crisp, freshly picked, $100 bills. "But I didn't complete my test. I didn't get you another picture."

Elyrise walked around the room and began to recite the familiar verse.

"Over the hills through the In Betweenz
You will discover what this task means.
Find answers long sought out
And bring back a treasure beyond a doubt."

As he spoke the last line, he stood behind Pierre and put his hand on his shoulder. Then he said, "You may recall that we were looking at the landscape painting from Pierre when I told you I required 'something else from this artist'."

Understanding hit Robbie like a blow to the head. He had not been searching for a painting, he had been searching for "something" more valuable, or "someone" long sought out. He was meant to find his father!

Elyrise was silent while he waited for Robbie to process the clues. Then Robbie explained it to the others in the room. "I assumed you wanted another painting from Pierre S., but you did not give me enough money to buy one. By letting me think you wanted another painting, you knew I would have to go directly to the artist himself. How did you know I would learn he was my father? How did **you** know he was my father?"

"The two of you have much in common. I had faith you would discover this."

"But why didn't you just tell me you knew my father?"

"You weren't ready, and I had to be sure."

A knock on the door announced another visitor. Goldie peeked her head in the door, "I thought I heard Robbie's voice." Robbie shifted as if to get up from the bed, but Goldie had already crossed the room and had her arms around Robbie. He embraced her back, this time without blushing, despite Pierre and Elyrise in the room.

Sitting on the bed next to him, Goldie asked quietly, "Now that you're awake, I guess you're anxious to get back home today?"

Robbie peered into the depths of Goldilock's eyes and thought about everything and everyone he would be leaving behind. "Yes," he replied, but his words did not match his tone.

Turning back toward Pierre, Robbie said, "There's just one thing more I need to do, before *we* can go home."

There was a shadow of doubt that crossed Pierre's face before he masked it. "I would love nothing more than to go home with you..." Pierre said recognizing the invitation. He paused as if there was more to add, but chose not to add it.

The moment was interrupted when more people bustled into the room. First came Blue, with a huge grin on his face. He was followed by Hansel and a healthy looking Gretel.

"Gretel! You're okay," Robbie exclaimed joyously.

Gretel quickly explained how Pegasus had flown her and Hansel to Elyrise, then Pegasus flew Blue to Eunice, the unicorn, who spared a few drops of her Unicorn blood as an antidote to the scorpion venom. After that, Gretel's recovery was speedy and they all waited at the Tree House for Robbie's return. Elyrise had moved to sit next to Gretel, one arm cradling her against his side like a doting grandfather. It was then that Robbie noticed Gretel playing with the beautiful amethyst pendant on her new necklace.

"I'm so glad everyone is okay. Now, I'm ready to see the Wizard so I can go home," Robbie said and everybody cheered.

"Almost, dear." Elyrisia had quietly entered the room with portable containers of food. Once again, Elyrise and his family were anticipating exactly what everybody needed. Elyrisia held up the bags of food and said, "Now, you are ready."

"You should have everything you need," Elyrison said as Pierre,

Robbie, Goldie, Blue, Hansel and Gretel crawled into Elyrise's very large horse-drawn carriage pulled by six white horses. "You should have enough food for the trip. You know Elyrisia. She packed tons of food. There are roasted ham sandwiches, freshly sliced roast beef sandwiches, pudding, macadamia nut cookies—I love macadamias. Where was I? Oh yes--grapes, strawberries, cheese sticks, fudge brownies. The coach driver's name is Melvin. He will take you wherever you need to go. There is no hurry to get the carriage back. We're not going anywhere soon, ha ha! We'll miss having you here. We love company—I could never have too much company. I think it's because we have the In-Betweenz on one side and the river on the other. And that London Bridge is always up and down. Oh yes, you're in luck—London Bridge is up right now. We just checked it this morning. Yes, Elyria loves to race the horses. She ran them down there and back while Robbie slept..."

Robbie was getting antsy to leave, but didn't want to be rude and interrupt Elyrison's endless monologue. Fortunately, the carriage driver knew better than to wait for the gale of words to blow itself out. He signaled to the horses and started the coach off with a dash while Elyrison was still mid-sentence. The travelers all leaned out the windows, waving and shouting their thanks and farewells.

London Bridge was indeed put back together, and the coach dashed over it quickly. There was no rain, no near drowning and no Big Bad Wolf on the return trip. Goldilocks spoke very little on the trip, but snuggled up to Robbie and fell asleep, while the coach approached the Wizard's place from the rear and avoided most of the poppy field.

The Wizard wasn't surprised when the group appeared at his gate. He greeted his old friend, Pierre with a warm embrace. Then Pierre introduced him to Robbie, as his son.

It wasn't the Wizard who was surprised, however; it was Pierre, for the Wizard just nodded and said, "I know

"Thine eyes have I seen once with mine.

A pair of two over this time.

Over the Human's Hills, below a peak,

There you will find what most you seek."

When he finished reciting, the Wizard looked back at the two pairs of lavender eyes with a knowing smile. Then lavender eyes turned to meet lavender eyes as both pairs began to look more silver than purple.

Pierre broke the silence, "I always knew the Wizard was a clever man."

Robbie now realized that the Wizard had recognized him as Pierre's son from the beginning. "Excuse me, sir," Robbie's anger gave him the courage to address the Wizard directly. "If you knew where my father was, why didn't you just tell me when we first met?"

"My dear young man, I didn't know your whole story and neither did you. It was for you to discover. I just started you on the first leg of your journey, which I knew would take you to Elyrise the Wise, particularly since you had this resourceful young man with you." The Wizard put his hand on Blue's shoulder.

"Me? I didn't know I was supposed to take him to Elyrise the Wise," Blue said, confused.

"Maybe you didn't know at first, but I knew he was in capable hands" the Wizard responded to Blue.

Hansel spoke up, "I was the one who first told him of the Forest of Money."

"Ah. Of course, that came from the intelligence of Hansel," acknowledged the Wizard.

Gretel spoke up. "I insisted on going to show him the way."

The Wizard ruffled her hair. "The brave little Gretel".

"I suppose he didn't need me at all," said Goldie disappointedly.

"On the contrary," spoke the Wizard. "I'm sure you were a true and faithful friend to him at all times."

Goldie blushed and was shocked that the Wizard seemed to know all of them so well, "but how did you know Robbie would find Pierre."

I told him where to look, of course, "I told him to look below the peak in the Human's Hills. Isn't that where you found Pierre?" The Wizard addressed the question to Robbie.

"Yes, but you could have been more direct," challenged Robbie.

"But, my boy, the best things in life don't always come easily. After all you have gained on your journey, do you now think it would have been better if I would have just sent for Pierre, introduced you and sent you back home the same day?"

Robbie slowly looked at each one of his new friends in turn, his gaze ending on his father, and acknowledged the wisdom of the Wizard.

The Wizard addressed Robbie again. "Now, you have made peace with your father, we must return you to your mother." The Wizard lowered his head and extended a graceful bow to the entire group before returning to his perch behind the curtain.

His head appeared, like a great spirit, on the huge stage in front of them. In a booming voice, the wizard dismissed them with yet another puzzling rhyme.

"Farewell my young friend,
Happiness does wait.
This is not the end.
Seek; that is your fate."

With Blue directing them, Melvin drove the coach back to the copse of trees beyond Blue's haystack and Robbie guided them as best he could after that. The group climbed out of the coach and unloaded the Transparency detector the Wizard's assistant had provided upon their departure. Blue commented that it was a shame they had to pay the Wizard the money when he so clearly had meant for the father and son to reunite, but Pierre had turned it over without hesitation, knowing that the Wizard has a reason for everything he does, and the money may be a key element in another adventure the Wizard was orchestrating.

The group started walking in the direction from which Robbie thought he had come, everyone hoping to find this invisible door. Robbie strained to remember any landmarks, but only recalled that he had walked some distance across the meadow before he had encountered Blue.

After a while, Robbie began to panic. Each endless view of the meadow seemed exactly the same.

Pierre put his arm across Robbie's shoulder, "It's okay son. We're all here to help, just try to remember."

"We have to be close," Robbie said to the group, feeling hopeless.

"Robbie can use the Transparency detector and the rest of us will fan out and search as we walk," Pierre instructed.

The group spread out like a search party, about four feet apart. Robbie was ahead of them, swinging the Transparency detector around in great sweeping motions as he had seen the contractor do. No sound could be heard except the air blowing from the fan, the diamond was not producing any holograms more interesting than stones and bugs.

"We've passed it. I'm sure we have," said Robbie desperately.

"Don't worry. We're going to find our way home," Pierre said

"*Home! We're going home! I'm going home, and Pierre is coming with me!*" Robbie thought and his excitement made him even more determined to find his door.

Robbie listened to the sound of the fan that the Wizard's assistant said would send air out a greater distance if the head of the fan were tilted out instead of down. Finally, he heard a different sound. It was a subtle resonating sound. There was no hologram so he must not be close enough to the object. He continued to walk forward in the direction the sound came from. Slowly, the sound got louder and more resonant. "I think I found something," Robbie said.

Blue broke out of formation and began running toward Robbie. "Ouch!" he said as he stopped to rub his head. "I do believe I just ran into something invisible." Then he smiled, and reached out his hand touching something solid...and invisible! Iridescent blue sparkled from each spot he touched on the invisible door.

"We found it!" Blue yelled to the others who came scrambling.

Now that the moment had come, Robbie knew he would have to say good-bye to all of his new friends. All but Pierre, whom he couldn't wait to take home to his mother. He wasn't looking forward to her initial reaction. She was likely to be mad as a hornet at him for disappearing for a week and even madder at Pierre for disappearing for 13 years! Maybe, he should leave Pierre in the graveyard until he had a chance to tell his mother the whole story.

Robbie turned to Hansel, who was standing nearest to him, and gave him a hearty handshake, "Thanks, man. I'm sorry for all the trouble I caused you, but it was great having you with us.

Gretel fell to the ground dramatically, sobbing that she would never see Robbie again. Robbie scooped her up and gave her a big kiss on her forehead. He gently put her down and put a hand to his heart, "You will always be with me here."

He choked on his words, unable to get any passed the tightness in his throat, as he tightly embraced Goldie. The tears were streaming down her face and it was all he could do to hold his own tears back.

When he got to Blue, he saw that Blue was smiling as usual.

"What?" Robbie asked a little surprised and deflated that Blue seemed so happy to see him go.

"Don't say goodbye, I'm going with you," Blue informed Robbie.

Robbie clapped Blue on the back with a big smile, then turned and caught the worried look on Pierre's face.

"I'm not sure what would happen if Blue went to the World Out There. Blue does not age here in the Land of Legends where he is a couple hundred years old. I have been here 13 years and I have not aged. But Robbie, you and I know that we age in the World Out There. I have been wondering if I will physically age 13 years the instant I step into the World Out There. If I do, will Blue instantly age a couple hundred years? That is sure to mean certain death for him."

The group looked somber for a minute. Robbie turned to Blue, "Sorry man. I really would have liked taking you home with me."

"Well, I'll just let Pierre go first. If he doesn't age instantly, then we know I'm safe." Blue said as he searched for the handle and yanked the door open.

"Fantastic!" said Blue pointing to the mausoleum and all the tombstones. "What is this place?"

"It's a cemetery and that's a mausoleum. It's where we bury people when they die," explained Robbie realizing that Blue would never have seen a cemetery in a land where no one ever dies.

"What's that noise and what's wrong with the sky and what's that smell?" Blue was enchanted by all the sights and sounds of the city. "What good is living for eternity if I can't have adventure?" Blue said and ducked through the door before Robbie could stop him.

The group gasped collectively, watching as they waited for Blue's body to turn to dust before their eyes. Blue made a choking sound, his eyeballs rolled up into his head and he fell down, convulsing and wheezing.

Gretel gasped and impulsively started to duck through the door to check on Blue, but Pierre reached out and grabbed her to rescue her from the same terrible death.

Then Blue sat up and opened his eyes, pointing to the group on the other side of the door. He laughed at them. "Got you. Look, I'm fine." To prove it, he stood up and danced a jig.

Blue's ridiculous dance broke the tension and made everyone laugh —everyone except Pierre who had moved in front of the door when he had reached for Gretel. There was no mask hiding the sorrow on his face now.

"Dad, what's wrong?" Robbie asked seeing the sadness on his father's face.

"I can't see it, Robbie. I can't see any of the things Blue described."

"It's okay, just follow me," Robbie said, and he grabbed Pierre's hand and leapt through the door. Robbie passed through easily, but Pierre vanished as he crossed the threshold.

"Dad!" Robbie yelled as he jumped back through the door into The Land of Legends where he saw Hansel, Gretel and Goldie, but still couldn't see his father. A moment later, Pierre emerged through Robbie's door. His eyes held large tears and his face was very pale.

"What happened? Where did you go?" Robbie choked out the words over the sudden dread he was feeling.

"Oh Robbie, I'm so sorry. I had hoped this wouldn't happen," Pierre said sadly. "The Wizard warned me a long time ago that the only way for me to leave the Land of Legends was to exit through the same door I entered. But my door was sealed shut. I didn't believe the Wizard and I continued to draw doors all the time, but each door I drew led me to a new world. I came back to Fairy Tale Town many, many times thinking that if I drew my doors in this place, they had to lead me back to Rosecrest, or at least to The World Out There. They never did...they always led to a new place. I burned each door I drew so that nobody would find them and be banished the way I have been banished. When you came, I hoped I could return home with you, back through the door you drew to the same world from the same location. But, no. All of you could see the cemetery. When I looked through your door, I saw a dark green sky and a barren ground with gaping holes. You went through your door to your world, and I ended up somewhere else.

"Robbie, I can't go with you. It has been such a joy to meet you, to get to know you. You are amazing. Know that I love you, son," Pierre embraced Robbie as both of them cried. "Tell your mother you found me. Tell her I love her, that I have always loved her. Tell her I am sorry that I was not with her all these years, but that I will never stop trying to find a way home."

"I can't leave you," Robbie sobbed.

"Think of your mother. You must go back." Pierre's voice was growing firmer. "Promise me you will not go on another adventure like this while your mother goes out of her mind with grief?"

All Robbie could do was nod his head.

"Now," Pierre said in a voice that faltered as he thrust Robbie's art case at him, "Turn around and go through that door. Keep it safe. Remember that is the only way for Blue to return home."

Robbie hung his head and turned around, but his feet would not move. He felt someone take his hand and looked up to see Goldie. She put her arm behind his back and urged him forward. She kept the pressure on his back as they stepped through the door and joined Blue in the cemetery.

"Thunk!" the trio heard as they turned to see the door had closed. Robbie searched for and found the handle, but the Land of Legends had shut them out.

The End

Follow Robbie and his friends through more adventures in book two:
LOL Life of Legends

Katy was born in Maryland. She has a long career as a school psychologist working with children of all ages. Writing fiction gives her a chance to escape the hectic pace of work. Katy also enjoys traveling to new places, exploring, hiking, biking, skiing, and playing pickleball. She loves the beach and the water, especially boating, kayaking, snorkeling, swimming or floating in a tube. She creates digital scrapbooks of her many adventures with family and friends. Katy started writing LOL: Land of Legends for her children, and the first edition was published in 2012. Life got busy and Katy finished the trilogy in 2020. Now, Katy's two children are grown and she lives in Florida with her husband.